Conservationists' Guide to Recycling Bridesmaid Dresses:

1. **Don't forget the tried-and-true quilt, particularly a wedding ring design.** It never hurts to have chartreuse lace and lime-green rayon reminders that the grass really wasn't greener on the single side.
2. **Place in steel garbage can and light match, hoping against hope that there aren't any flame-retardant materials.** (Oops, wrong list.)
3. **Make decorative trashcan liners.** They will add color to your bathroom scheme while keeping your princess-waist, tea-length fashion faux pas where it really belongs.
4. **Hang in back of closet as a conversation piece.** Clearly the most popular choice, the hoarding practice will someday give your teenage daughter proof that your clothes were more ridiculous than hers.
5. **Sew several together as a kite.** Whenever you fly it, you'll announce the lengths you were willing to go—even to look like a periwinkle mushroom—all in the name of forever love.

Books by Dana Corbit

Love Inspired

A Blessed Life #188
An Honest Life #233
A New Life #274
A Family for Christmas #278
"Child in a Manger"
On the Doorstep #316
Christmas in the Air #322
"Season of Hope"
A Hickory Ridge Christmas #374
Flower Girl Bride #394

DANA CORBIT

started telling "people stories" at about the same time she started forming words. So it came as no surprise when the Indiana native chose a career in journalism. As a newspaper reporter and features editor, Dana told true-life stories of wonderful everyday people. She left the workforce to raise her children, but the stories came home with her as she discovered the joy of writing fiction. The nationally award-winning journalist feels blessed to have the opportunity to share the stories of her heart with readers.

Dana, who makes her home in southeast Michigan, balances the make-believe realm of her characters with her equally exciting real-life world as a wife, carpool coordinator for three athletic daughters and food supplier for two disinterested felines.

Flower Girl Bride

Dana Corbit

Published by Steeple Hill Books™

STEEPLE HILL BOOKS

ISBN-13: 978-0-373-87430-9
ISBN-10: 0-373-87430-8

FLOWER GIRL BRIDE

This edition published by arrangement with Steeple Hill Books.

www.SteepleHill.com

Printed in U.S.A.

Trust in the Lord with all your heart,
and do not rely on your own insight.
In all your ways acknowledge Him,
and He will make straight your paths.
—*Proverbs* 3:5-6

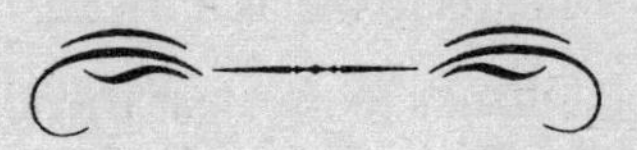

To our sweet second daughter, Caterina, who always views the world as an open doorway of possibilities and who gives those of us around her the gift of her contagious smile. Also to Cindy Thomas and Sandy Morris, who have welcomed me as a neighbor and opened their hearts to me as a friend.

A special thanks to my dear friend, speech pathologist Maija Anderson, for her insights into her profession. Thanks also to the employees of the Starbucks store in Northville, Michigan, who didn't throw me out when I discovered that this story flowed best with a vanilla latte, a molasses cookie and all that delicious white noise.

Chapter One

I will be happy for Aunt Eleanor and Uncle Jack, I vowed, repeating the words like a mantra, as I drove toward the beach house where they were hosting their own silver anniversary party. That the party came complete with a renewal of vows ceremony only made me strengthen my own promise.

Usually, I avoided all things nuptial because they only provided painful reminders of my own failed marriage, but today wasn't about me. No matter how ugly my scars, I was determined not put a damper on my aunt and uncle's special day.

Lake Michigan winked out at me from between modest homes and mansions as I followed the winding road toward Bluffton Point Lighthouse. Even through the dusty windshield, the water appeared glassy smooth, its color deepening in stripes from sky blue to violet.

In the distance, the redbrick lighthouse stood majestically, peering down at its kingdom and offering protection to seasoned fishermen and novice recreational boaters alike.

The siren call of these surroundings, which lulled visitors into the slow-paced vacation mindset of Mantua, Michigan, helped to lift my mood—or would have if I hadn't been so uncomfortably warm.

Brushing at the sweat trickling down my neck, I grumbled over my car's air-conditioning unit, which desperately needed a shot of refrigerant. If only I'd remembered to include that in my summer break budget, but as it was, I'd be sweating it out until school started the last week of August.

This was supposed to be the first week of June near one of the Great Lakes, not the South Atlantic. As I sat with the backs of my legs sticking to the upholstery, nothing could convince me that Michigan hadn't slipped south of the equator.

My cell phone picked that moment to cue up "Pop Goes the Weasel" and give me another reminder to read the owner's manual and learn how to change the ring. Pulling over on the shoulder of the road, I reached down for the phone in the passenger seat, flipped it open and pressed it to my ear.

"Cassie, sweetheart, is that you?" Eleanor Hudson nearly shouted into the receiver before I had the chance to say hello.

"Of course it's me, Aunt Eleanor. You called me, remember?"

"Watch yourself, missy. You know, you shouldn't be talking on your cell phone while you're driving."

I smiled for the first time all day. Dad had always

said that even the Grinch couldn't stay in a bad mood around his sister. "Guess you don't know me as well as you think. I pulled over before picking up the phone, but I'm not getting there any faster by sitting here."

"Sorry, sweetie." Her cheery voice didn't sound all that apologetic. "I've got pre-wedding jitters. I need my favorite niece to help me get through it."

"I'm your only niece on both sides, right?"

"Well..." What could only have been a middle-aged woman's giggle came through the line.

"Aunt Eleanor," I started again. "I don't know what you're worried about. Uncle Jack is still nuts about you, even after twenty-five years. Otherwise, how could you have convinced him to be a part of this off-the-wall vows renewal thing?"

The idea was wild, all right, with a ceremony right on the beach. How was that repeating history, anyway? The first time my aunt and uncle had spoken their vows, they'd been standing in a tiny country church outside Waterloo. There were pictures to prove it.

"I have ways of convincing him." With barely a pause, Eleanor asked, "When should we expect you? Princess is dying to meet you."

"I'm sure she is." Not that I was convinced that cats became excited about anything, let alone houseguests. I'd heard tales about Princess for the last few years, but this was the first time I would make her royal acquaintance. I wondered if my aunt would expect me to curtsy when I did.

"Everyone else is already here, too. The whole wedding party. Even—"

"Great." I cut her off before she could give a list of strangers' names. At this rate, I would never get there. "I'm looking forward to it."

I hoped the last statement conveyed my enthusiasm for this time and for the couple I adored. My aunt and uncle had every right to expect me to be thrilled over their silver wedding anniversary. And I was.

On the other hand, this marriage renewal *event* didn't exactly give me the urge to turn cartwheels and shake pom-poms. The party would celebrate enduring love and commitment. My own experience of it had been as much a fallacy as it was fleeting. Hardly the stuff that dreams were made of.

Because this party felt like an in-your-face commentary on my failures, I had planned to arrive early and fade inconspicuously into the walls of my aunt and uncle's lake cottage. My stalling had messed up even those good intentions, and now everyone would think I had arrived fashionably late to make an entrance when all I wanted was an excuse for an exit.

After saying goodbye to Aunt Eleanor, I continued to follow her directions to the address on the invitation. When I thought I was there, I slowed the car, but I already knew it wasn't the right place. The sprawling, blond-brick structure had a huge entry arch, tons of windows and was probably insulated with bundles of cash.

I couldn't imagine my aunt and uncle moving to a place like this. Most of their marriage, they'd lived happily in a modest ranch house near Jackson.

Still, the numbers matched. Apparently, *The Millionaire Next Door* had nothing on my relatives.

Almost as soon as I pulled into the driveway, Eleanor leaned into the open driver's-side door and gave me a fierce hug. Chin-length hair that she kept its lovely champagne color by maintaining strict six-week touch-ups fluttered across my cheek. Her comforting warmth enveloped me, which felt strange at first, because I hadn't felt warm inside all year.

"Cassandra Eleanor." Like always, she used my first and middle names to remind anyone listening that I was her namesake.

"Hi, Aunt Eleanor," I said into her shoulder. "You said *cottage*, not *mansion*."

Her chest rumbled against me with her chuckle. "No, I believe I said *house*. Just wait until you see the view from the deck. God gave us front-row seats to every West Michigan sunset."

Kindly, my aunt didn't mention that I would have seen their view and met their precious Princess before if I'd visited any time since they'd moved in three summers before. I'd been far too busy messing up my own life to be involved in anyone else's.

Aunt Eleanor pulled back so I could stand up, but she didn't release me completely. I hoped she wouldn't because I might have been tempted to cling.

"You're a sight for sore eyes."

She had that right. I was a sight, and I probably made her eyes sore. I held my breath, waiting for her to comment on my weight, which was a good ten pounds below the one hundred twenty-five where I looked my best. But she didn't mention that or the raccoon eyes that my liquid concealer failed to hide.

Maybe mothers were the only ones who felt obliged to point out weight gains or losses, bad haircuts and unfortunate wardrobe choices. Funny, I missed even those things now that the death dates were filled in on both sides of Mom and Dad's joint headstone.

My only remaining blood relative on my father's side drew me into her arms, though now that I was standing, I had to bend at the waist to let her reach up to me.

"Well, Ellie, are you going to let the rest of us get a look at Cassie or not?"

Jack Hudson appeared beside his wife, wearing his familiar toothy grin under his graying mustache, plus a potbelly he'd further developed in the last few years. His hug was every bit as tight my aunt's as he spoke with a muffled voice into my rat's nest of blond hair. I should have known better than to leave the car window open if I didn't tie my hair back.

"You get prettier every day."

Today I knew that was a fib, though he'd said it to me dozens of times before. I could hear other voices, but I couldn't see past my uncle's sizable height and girth.

It was just as well since I wouldn't know any of these people I would be expected to remember, anyway. I didn't want to hear someone say, "Last time I saw you, you were this big," as they held their hands at about waist height. If I heard that, I might be tempted to spout off that the last time I saw them their hair wasn't so gray. That probably wouldn't earn me any Brownie points.

I especially didn't want to hear about how adorable I'd been in the pictures of the original wedding with the little ring bearer—Lucky or something. Since he wasn't related to either the bride or the groom and wouldn't feel obligated to attend this cutesy event, I probably wouldn't have to pretend to know him at all.

Though I wished I could remember for Aunt Eleanor's sake, I could recall only a few fuzzy details of the day I pranced down the aisle as her flower girl. If only my memory could be as blissfully vague over my own fiasco of a wedding and marriage.

"Let her breathe, Jack. I'm about to get jealous."

My uncle's laughter boomed at that. "And well you should. She's not little Miss Cassie Blake anymore."

And never would be again, I was tempted to announce as my uncle stepped back to reveal a sea of smiling faces. My name wouldn't even *be* Blake if I hadn't asked for it back while negotiating for my car and grandma's piano in the divorce.

I could no more picture this Cassandra Whittinger—this Mrs. Alan Whittinger—than I could see myself as that little blond darling with ringlet curls who had worn a periwinkle taffeta dress with crinolines to the wedding. I was no longer that nearly five-year-old girl who had mimicked the bride and groom by sharing a buttercream-icing-flavored kiss with the ring bearer under the table. I was just weeks away from my thirtieth birthday, and I felt even older than that.

"Cassie, dear, are you paying attention?"

"Hmm?" I turned back to my aunt's softly rounded image. Like her husband, Aunt Eleanor had blossomed a bit since her big day as the blushing bride. "I'm sorry. What were you saying?"

Aunt Eleanor came forward and rested both warm hands on my forearms. "Sweetie, you look exhausted after such a long drive. We can wait until after you've rested for you to become reacquainted with everyone else."

She made it sound as if I'd passed through three time zones and required a passport for my journey from Toledo, but I nodded anyway, grateful for the reprieve. Maybe I could get through this weekend after all. Just a few days of smiling, and it all would be over. I could do that.

The sacrifices were small for the reward at the end: three weeks of solitude at my aunt and uncle's cottage-slash—mansion—slash—house. Well, near solitude anyway. Princess would be there, too, but she was probably one of those aloof cats that wouldn't notice I was around as long as I kept food in her bowl. How hard could it be?

Anyway, I knew full well that Aunt Eleanor had asked me to cat-sit when she could just as easily have asked a neighbor to pull cat duty. I recognized emotional charity when I heard it, yet I was in no position to turn it down. Nearly two years had passed since the divorce, and I was still in get-through-the-day mode.

What I needed was a break in the routine, and a few weeks on Michigan's incredible west coast might be just the ticket. I would sink my toes in the sand and wait for the sun to draw the highlights out in my hair. I would let the water and a dozen or so of the sunsets my aunt had promised lull me out of the lethargy that had become my life. Maybe surrounded by God's creation, I would even be inspired to pray a little again.

Worry creased my aunt's eyebrows when I glanced at her, but her expression softened as she smiled.

"You're right," I told her. "I am pretty tired."

I gave a quick wave to the crowd. "I look forward to meeting—I mean *seeing* all of you again—later." Nobody stared me down or accused me of being a coward, so I figured I had passed that test.

As Aunt Eleanor slipped away to attend to her other guests, Uncle Jack stepped forward and squeezed my shoulder. "You rest a little. There'll be plenty of time for visiting tonight at the rehearsal dinner."

Rehearsal dinner? They were taking this whole second-wedding thing a little *too* seriously as far as I was concerned.

My uncle must have sensed my incredulity because he chuckled then. "There's no real rehearsal. We promise. We're planning to wing it tomorrow, but this gives us an excuse for another big meal." He patted his rounded stomach. "Any excuse is good enough for me."

Jack turned back to Eleanor and the crowd that was beginning to disperse. "Ellie, are we going to show Cassie to her room?"

I glanced at the garage's side entry. Maybe Aunt Eleanor would take me in that way, like family, rather than through the front door as a guest. A wave of sadness rushed over me as I thought about how long it had been since I'd been with family, since I'd felt at home.

"In just a minute," my aunt called out from behind me. "But before I do, I want to make just one introduction—I mean *re*introduction."

"Ellie I'd wait—" Uncle Jack began, but I waved my hand to interrupt him.

"No, that's fine." Slowly, I turned back to where the crowd had been.

Standing next to Aunt Eleanor but with his attention focused on someone on the other side of the crowd was a man with dark, wavy hair and a pleasant face. He towered above my aunt, not much of a feat since even at my five feet eight I had her by a few inches. I tried to place him, but he didn't look like anyone from the wedding picture in my wall collage. He was too young to have been among them anyway.

Eleanor cleared her throat. "Cassie, I'd like you to meet a friend of mine."

The man turned his head and looked right at me. His eyes were huge, startling and royal blue. He had those thick, spiky eyelashes that I always envied in men and resented as I painted and curled my own pale lashes. His eyes, though, were incredible. They were so familiar, so— And suddenly I knew.

With a flourish of her hand, Eleanor indicated the man. "I'd like to present former ring bearer, now all-grown-up Luke Sheridan."

Dumbstruck. That's the only way I could describe the jumble of feelings inside me as I just stood there staring up at Luke, my mouth hanging open like an invitation for West Michigan's black flies. My cheeks were so hot that I must have looked as if I had a killer sunburn, and I hadn't so much as made it out to the beach.

The guy standing across from me looked annoyingly

composed while I was well on my way to collapsing in a heap of humiliation. His posture was stiff, though, and his eyes widened, his pupils contracting in the bright sunlight. He had tanned, weather-roughed skin to hide his embarrassment, but he had to feel as ridiculous as I did.

The rest of the crowd stood behind him silently, looking back and forth between the two of us as if they were waiting for something to happen. I'd so been set up, and I hadn't even seen it coming. What did these people expect, that they could throw us together and start a bunch of fireworks? We weren't little kids anymore.

"Luke, you remember Cassie," Aunt Eleanor said, breaking the silence.

He studied my face for several seconds. His gaze moved from the cat-green eyes I'd inherited from my mother to the spattering of freckles across my nose. He paused briefly on my mouth, which I'd finally managed to close, before he turned back to his hostess.

"Sure," he said, probably to humor my aunt.

Who remembered people they met before their fifth birthday, anyway? Well, obviously I did, but I couldn't be counted as normal by any stretch of the word. Come to think of it, I didn't remember much else about *being* five, even my own fifth birthday party a few weeks after my aunt's wedding. Like the wedding, I knew about that day mostly from the pictures my mother kept in organized albums.

"How's it going?" He stepped forward and jutted out his hand.

I blinked a few times but somehow managed to grip his hand for a civil greeting before pulling away again.

"Good...ah...to see you again."

"You probably remember me as Lucky."

Lucky. That was probably how the women who dated him described themselves. I blinked. Now that thought had come out of left field, and I didn't even like baseball.

I tried to clear my throat and my head at the same time. "I was just Cassie...when you met me, I mean." I couldn't seem to control the wrestling match my hands were having at my waist.

He lifted an eyebrow. "Then hi again, *just* Cassie."

As soon as he said it, Luke's gaze darted over to someone in the crowd, his eyes narrowing. My stomach tightened, as I imagined his wife or fiancée or girlfriend cowering among the faces, a third party to this fiesta of humiliation.

"Luke's Clyde Lewis's right-hand man in Heritage Hill Real Estate Development," Aunt Eleanor told me. "They're developers for the new Wings Gate subdivision near Shelby. Those places make this old house look like a beach shack."

I nodded dumbly at my aunt's sales job. What was I supposed to say, "Going once, going twice, sold?" She didn't mention my career at all, so I guessed she didn't think it would properly impress.

Luke turned back to Eleanor. "You said Cassie was tired. I'm sure we'll all have a chance to talk later."

He'd taken pity on me, and it shamed me how grateful I felt for such a small gesture of kindness. That I couldn't remember the last time a man had done anything so nice for me only emphasized how empty my social life had been since the divorce.

Eleanor nodded, her shoulders curled forward and her lips pressed together. Had she really expected that Luke would sweep me off my feet and march right off to the altar or something? Well, I hated to disappoint her, but I was no longer the sweeping type. I might still be a romantic movie lover, new and old, but that didn't mean I believed the *It Could Happen to You* idea.

"It was nice meeting you," I said, already taking a step back.

"Meeting?" someone in the crowd called out. "You two are old friends."

The frown Luke shot over his shoulder must have been effective at cutting off additional comments because only a few nervous titters followed.

Eleanor's shoulders perked up again, and she reached for his hand with one of hers and for mine with the other. "Does anyone remember these two at our wedding? I was almost jealous of them, stealing so much attention on my big day. They were so cute."

Luke gently extracted his hand. "I'm sure we were, but that was a long time ago."

Eleanor released my hand and reached up to brush back my messy hair. "Does anyone remember those ringlet curls?"

"Or the amount of hair gel it required to tame a little-boy cowlick?"

That came from a middle-aged brunette who had to be Luke's mother. I didn't remember her, either, but I'd often heard stories about my aunt's best friend, Yvonne Sheridan.

"Or those kisses," called out the anonymous person in the crowd.

Luke turned to the others again, and his jaw tightened.

"Those two were inseparable that whole weekend," a dark-headed man in the back said. "Wherever you found one you found the other."

"That was twenty-five years ago," Luke said with a warning finality.

Given the opening, I jumped on it. "Yeah, let's hear it for Jack and Eleanor. Twenty-five years. Here's to twenty-five more." I started clapping, encouraged when the rest of the crowd joined me. Soon someone executed a perfect two-finger whistle, and a couple of others were whooping in my aunt and uncle's honor.

"Hip-hip hooray," Luke called out, raising his arm into the air.

When our gazes connected briefly, the side of his mouth pulled up in a silly half grin. I ignored the equally silly tremor inside my belly. Had it really been that long since an attractive man had smiled at me?

My uncle must have taken the lull in conversation as his cue to step in and contain his effervescent wife because he placed an arm around Eleanor's shoulder.

"Okay, everyone. That's enough torturing of the guests. This is supposed to be a fun weekend for all of us, and these two aren't having much fun."

Luke appeared as if he wanted to hug Uncle Jack, but I beat him to it. I wrapped my arms around my warm, wonderful uncle and pressed my cheek to his shoulder.

"See you all later." I nearly dragged Uncle Jack through the side door.

I expected to feel relief as the door closed behind me, but a strange disappointment filled me instead. Had I expected something to happen just as my would-be matchmakers obviously had? Clearly, I'd been spending too much time reading "Cinderella" and watching *It's a Wonderful Life.*

No, I was way too sensible to be waiting for knights on white horses or invitations to royal balls. I should have been angrier with my aunt for trying to set me up in the first place. I was fine. I was a modern divorcée with an apartment decorated just the way I liked it and a career in speech pathology that challenged and fulfilled me. I had everything I needed.

So why did that niggling seed of discontent dig under the sand of my consciousness and refuse to flutter off in the breeze? Why did it make me question if something was missing in my life?

Chapter Two

"This place is amazing."

I glanced around the mammoth great room of my aunt and uncle's lakeside home, taking in the floor-to-ceiling windows, the honey-oak-colored wood floors and the comfortable furniture groupings. With walls and accents painted in warm earth tones, thick area rugs and sofas and loveseats so deep and plush that they practically begged for someone to nap on them, the place was a decorator's showplace that doubled as a retreat.

In the far end of the great room, there was a television so big that watching my movies on it would feel like a night at the cinema. I could almost taste the butter popcorn already.

"Yeah, we like it," my uncle said.

Jack smiled as he stared up at the circular stairway leading to the second floor. On the wall beyond it, which stretched to the upper level, was a series of paintings of Michigan lighthouses. In one of those paintings, I recognized the redbrick Bluffton Point Lighthouse, the one that stood just down the beach.

"If I lived in a place like this, I'd never want to leave home."

"Then maybe it was a mistake for us to have you house-sit. You'll be the guest who never leaves."

"I'll leave, I promise. As soon as you two get back from Paris."

"Okay then. The guest suite is upstairs. Third door on the right."

"Suite? Hey, this is my kind of roughing it."

"That just means it has its own head."

I nodded, somehow managing to keep a straight face. Living in a fancy house or not, my uncle was the same humble man who'd spent one summer of his youth working on a fishing boat crew and still used the lingo.

Jack started for the door. "You go ahead on up. I'll pull in your car and bring in your bags."

I looked up the stairs and then back at him. Though I didn't remember having handed them to him, my car keys dangled from his fingers. "You don't need to…" But he waved away my argument and disappeared through the door to the garage.

Shrugging, I climbed the stairs, crossed to the third closed door and pushed it open. The room inside was a little too fussy for my taste. I might have selected the same rich wood armoire, bureau and four-poster bed if I came into some unexpected inheritance, but I would have skipped the flowery bedspread and those matching, frilly, tieback curtains. And the pillows…why did anybody need a dozen white lace pillows on any bed?

I stepped closer to get a better look at them. Maybe their appeal would jump out at me upon closer inspection.

Something jumped out, all right.

Crouched among the pillows was a runt-sized cat, staring at me with eyes as green as mine. I stiffened, but managed not to squeal the way I usually did when something startled me. Good thing. As tense as the cat appeared trapping me in its wary stare, it probably would have shot straight into the air.

No wonder I'd missed seeing the critter at first among the pillows. The cat's white fur matched the material, except for one black front paw and a few other tiny black speckles on its back.

"Hi, kitty," I said, in what I hoped was a soothing voice. I took a tentative step forward.

The cat only jumped back and hissed at me.

I backed up a few steps toward the door. Could this wild creature possibly be my aunt and uncle's precious cat? From the way they'd described her, I would have expected some froufrou feline like a chocolate Persian or a lilac point Himalayan, not this feral mixed breed spitting and hissing in the middle of my bed. The cat's back arched so high that it nearly folded itself into an upside-down U, and every hair on its stubby tail stood on end.

My hand touched the door behind me. I'd never been the hero type, and this was probably as good a time as any to beat a hasty retreat.

"I see you've met our Princess." Uncle Jack pressed past me into the room and set my suitcase and my duffel bag on the floor next to the bed.

He clucked his tongue at the cat. "Now, Princess, I've been looking all over for you. You must have got yourself locked in here this morning." He looked back and forth between his pet and me and then frowned at the cat. "Is that any way to treat our guest?"

By degrees, Princess returned from that distorted form, though keeping a wary eye on me.

Jack scooped up the cat in his arms and rubbed beneath her chin. Princess rewarded him by purring loudly.

"You see she's just a pussycat. Not a tiger like she was letting on." He smiled over at me. "Don't worry. She'll warm up to you."

Somehow I doubted that, but I didn't speak up for fear the cat would leap out of his arms with claws bared.

He scratched the cat's tiny white ears and crooned to it again. "How about you and I go downstairs and let Cassie here get some rest?"

Because Princess didn't seem to disagree, he carried her out of the room. "We'll see you a little later," he said over his shoulder.

I closed the door behind him and slumped down on the bed. This weekend was getting worse and worse. First, the scene with Luke Sheridan and now this. How was I supposed to take care of that cat when it clearly hated me on sight? Well, I had better get used to the inside of this room because the little monster would probably hold me hostage until my aunt and uncle returned from their second honeymoon.

Just as I was tracing a burgundy-colored pencil line over one half of my upper lip, a heavy knock came at the door to my guest suite. My hand jerked, sending the dark line past the corner of my mouth and making it look as if I'd drawn on a smile. Hey, that didn't sound like a bad idea, but I doubted I could pull off the look without matching it with clown-white makeup, a polka-dot outfit and size-eighteen shoes.

"Cassie, are you almost ready?" Aunt Eleanor called from outside the door. "We need to leave for the restaurant in about five minutes."

"I'll be right out." As gently as possible so as not to leave a huge red mark, I rubbed off the line, repairing the spot with a bit more concealer and a dusting of powder.

I finished lining my lips and applied lipstick before examining the results in the mirror. The simple black sheath dress hung on what was left of my curves, and its dark color against my too-pale skin made me look a little like Morticia Addams on a hunger strike.

It wasn't great, that was for sure, but compared to the way I'd looked when I'd closed myself in this room two hours before, this transformation might have been one for the record books. *Dud to decent in a duo of hours.* I'd even wrestled my hair into one of those fancy updos that my stylist was always encouraging me to try.

If she were still alive, Mom would have asked me why I was trying so hard to impress these people when I'd already made a less than spectacular first impression. Mom had believed first impressions were critical. They ranked second in importance only to clean underwear in case I was in an accident and needed the Jaws of Life to pull me from a burning car.

Technically, though, I'd met all of these people

twenty-five years before, so the first-impression argument was moot. And since they'd already seen me in my traveling worst, I just wanted to show them that I could at least clean up nice.

My traitorous subconscious asked if there were any particular guests I was trying to impress, but I shut down the thought as absurd. I just didn't want to embarrass my aunt and uncle at the party, and that was that.

Besides, a thought like that would suggest that I had given more than passing notice to Luke Sheridan, and I wasn't about to admit that, even under the threat of torture.

Men like that one, with patrician features and enough thick, wavy hair to soften them, not to mention those eyes that were surely the inspiration for the color "royal" in the crayon box, probably drew all kinds of female attention. He was just going to have to live without my entering his fan club.

Thanks, but no thanks, Aunt Eleanor. I didn't plan to get back into the dating game anytime soon.

I took one more peek in the mirror. Well, the image hadn't improved in the last forty-five seconds, so I hurried across the room in case the whole getup might revert to rags even before the stroke of midnight. On the way through the door, I snagged my sequined evening bag, filled to capacity with a twenty-dollar bill, driver's license, tube of lipstick and a roll of breath mints.

The last thing I wanted was to show up late and be the center of attention again. I'd had enough fun playing bug-under-the-microscope for one day. Someone else needed to take a turn, and I would be thrilled if it turned out to be the couple represented by the wedding cake topper.

Aunt Eleanor waited for me when I descended the stairs to the landing. "Well, don't you look lovely, sweetheart."

"Thanks, but no one could compare to you tonight. You look positively radiant."

She batted her eyelashes and twirled, the full skirt of her peach chiffon dress fluttering around her like one of the "spinny" dresses I used to wear to Sunday school. Her dress was probably designed for a mother-of-the-bride to blend with some daughter's unfortunate choice of wedding colors, but it was a perfect match for my aunt's peaches-and-cream complexion.

"I should argue with you, but I won't." Her laughter filtered over me before she reached up and brushed my cheek.

Eleanor glanced toward the door. "We'd better get out there. Everyone's waiting on us."

Again? I tried to cover my sigh with a cough. My aunt turned to study me, her eyes narrowed. "You're not coming down with something, are you? If you are, you should march right back upstairs—"

I wasn't sure why, but I waved my hand to interrupt her. She'd made it easy for me to back out on tonight, but I couldn't bring myself to grab the dangling carrot.

"No, I'm fine. Really. Let's get going."

"Okay. Tomorrow we'll have the bus to take us to the reception, but tonight we're taking our own cars."

When we stepped outside, several vehicles were already lined up along the road, and a few more were parked in the drive. I glanced around to find my own, but then I remembered that my uncle had parked my car in one of the garage's three stalls and hadn't returned the keys.

"I guess I'll ride with you then," I said with more than a little hope in my voice. At least if I rode with my relatives, I wouldn't have to face another embarrassing moment like the one earlier.

But my aunt shook her head. "Barb and Tom insisted that Jack and I ride in the lead car, and Tom's midlife-crisis convertible barely fits the four of us."

I nodded, glancing around and hoping for an obvious place to squeeze in, but all the cars looked like cramped quarters as far as I could tell. "Speaking of fitting, where are you going to put all of these people tonight? I didn't see any place to stay but a campground when I was driving in."

Already, I could picture myself sharing that queen-size guest bed with someone's aunt or sister who snored. Or worse yet, I would probably end up relegated to the floor only to share a room with a sleepwalker.

"Oh, didn't I tell you?" Eleanor held her hands wide the way she always did when she had what she called a "blond moment." "Our neighbors here are great. Several have offered their guest rooms, and the few who were going to be out of town opened their homes to us."

"You do have great neighbors. You know, I could pull my car out and follow."

"Nonsense." She brushed away my suggestion with a wave of her hand, glancing down the line of cars. She stopped as her gaze landed on a newer heavy-duty truck, painted a metallic blue. "Of course. You can ride in the truck."

I was already shaking my head over trying to find a ladylike way to haul myself into the pickup when the driver turned back from whatever held his attention in the backseat. A head full of dark hair came into view. I didn't need that quiver in my stomach to convince me I'd been had again, but there it was.

Aunt Eleanor, bless her heart, had the grace to look guilty.

Peeking to make sure the window was closed, I turned back to her. "I suppose there's no room in the other cars?"

"Doesn't look like it."

No one could have mistaken my exasperated sigh for an attempt to enjoy the Lake Michigan breeze. I wanted to be civil, but these people really needed a hobby that didn't involve my nonexistent love life.

"Look, Aunt Eleanor, I appreciate your concern for me, but dating is so far from what I want to be doing right now. I'm not ready—"

"Dating? Who said anything about dating?"

My aunt waggled her eyebrow as if I'd been the one to come up with the idea. I'd never had an unkind thought about my aunt in my life, but I had an overwhelming urge to trip her.

Still, the mental picture of her landing like a fallen butterfly, all tied up in layers of filmy peach chiffon, was enough to help me keep my feet to myself. *What would Jesus do?* the lukewarm, on-the-fence faith nugget inside of me wanted to know. I had a pretty good idea tripping wouldn't be part of His plan.

"I was just talking about a ride to dinner, but if you'd

rather I rearrange everyone else..." She let her words trail away, looking at me as if she hoped I would cave.

And I did. "No, of course, I don't want to inconvenience anyone."

Why would I start now? I had a track record for being one of the least inconveniencing people I knew. I hated to make waves. But I was a little desperate here, so I tried one last plea.

"I'm a bit uncomfortable riding alone with a man, though." I held my breath and crossed all twenty fingers and toes in my imagination.

I could practically see the wheels in her mind turning, as if she was trying to decide whether to take pity on me. Then she clapped her hands together. "Well, that's great then because you won't be riding with Luke alone. He's never alone."

Never alone? She didn't even give me time to ask that question aloud or to feel humiliated over learning this late in the game that Luke Sheridan might be happily married after all. In a chiffon flounce, she stepped to the truck and whipped open the door.

Luke first glanced over in surprise before his gaze landed on me and narrowed. It was all I could do not to throw my hands up in a pose of the innocent and tell him I had nothing to do with this.

"Luke, dear, would you mind transporting a guest to the restaurant? It seems we don't have a spot for my niece."

"Well, we couldn't have that, could we?" His tone was polite, but his jaw was tight.

Embarrassment had to be what was squeezing my chest so tightly. That and a huge slice of humble pie.

"Who's that?" came a youthful voice from the backseat.

Though both my aunt and I ducked to get a glimpse behind Luke, only she waved and grinned at the little boy sitting in a booster.

"Hello there, Sam," Eleanor said. "Are you taking good care of your daddy?"

I blinked hard, but at least I didn't really embarrass myself by gasping or saying, "oh." I'd considered that Luke might be married and realized now that I must have imagined this whole setup scenario, but I hadn't yet leaped as far as the progeny question.

The mini-Luke—no, Mr. Sheridan couldn't deny fathering this handsome knockoff if both their lives depended on it—was too busy studying me to answer my aunt's question.

Luke cleared his throat. "Um, Sam…Mrs. Hudson asked you something."

A scowl clouded Sam's handsome face. "Daddy made me wear this stuff."

He pointed down at an outfit that anyone besides a little boy would have called casual. It must have been a travesty to have to wear dressy tan shorts—oh the horror!—and a polo shirt with a collar.

But in the way of preschoolers, Sam must have forgotten this crime against his person because he grinned when he looked back at me. "Are you daddy's girlfriend?"

"Samuel Lucas Sheridan." Luke's voice came in a low, warning growl.

Sam glanced at his dad with a "what-did-I-say" look. The kid had guts, all right.

"Well, Grammy said—"

"I don't care what—" Luke stopped himself and took a deep breath before he continued. "I mean your grandma must have been joking because you know I don't have girlfriends."

"Mommy was your girlfriend."

Again, Luke's voice was low with warning. "We don't need to talk about this now."

"Well, she was."

Luke sighed. "Yes, she was."

Satisfied with his father's admission, Sam turned those enormous blue eyes, so like his father's, on me. "Mommy died."

My breath caught, the truth so bluntly laid out before me. Here I'd been worrying about, first, being set up and, second, mistakenly assuming I'd been set up, and this poor little boy had lost his mother. Shame felt heavy on my chest.

"I'm so sorry," I said when I finally had my voice back.

"Thanks," Luke said automatically. "Car accident. It was a while ago."

Not long enough for the pain to become less raw, I observed, as his hands tightened around the steering wheel. I had once told myself it would have been easier if Alan had just died instead of leaving me. Divorce was a death of sorts—of promises and dreams. But the stark look of loss on Luke's face suggested more pain than I could even fathom. He pointedly looked away then, making it clear he wasn't interested in my pity.

"Guys, we need to get going," Eleanor said as she put a hand in the small of my back and propelled me forward. Instantly, I was glad Luke drove a truck. Had it been a car, I would have clipped my head on the doorframe. As it was, the side of the seat just caught me in the stomach, making the air whoosh out of me. Scrambling for balance, I somehow ended up in the seat next to Luke without collecting any visible marks.

"See you all at the restaurant," Aunt Eleanor called out as she closed the door behind me.

Sam's head bobbed over the back of the seat before his dad had pulled into the traffic lane.

"Hey, lady, what's your name?"

Luke looked sharply over his shoulder. "Sam, what did we discuss about you unbuckling your safety seat?"

"You said it's dangerous."

"Then could you please tell me what you're doing out of the harness?"

A chuckle rumbled in my throat, and I pressed my lips together to keep from grinning. Nobody could say that young Sam Sheridan didn't listen when his dad spoke. Now following his advice, he hadn't quite mastered that one. His dad might have been a stick-in-the-mud, but I had no doubt Sam and I would be fast friends. I'd never met a kid I didn't like, and I could tell already that Sam Sheridan wouldn't be my first. Adults were a different story.

"Back in the harness, and I want to hear two clicks right away," Luke told him.

Sam made a face only his father could love, but he clicked one buckle and then the other.

When order had returned inside the vehicle, I peered over the seat at Sam. "Oh, you asked my name. It's Cassandra Blake, but you may call me Cassie."

"Make that Miss Cassie," Luke corrected.

"Of course."

I smiled at Sam when my expression was really targeted at his father. I felt inordinately pleased that Luke was trying to instill a respect for adults in his son, a lesson that some of my students hadn't learned at home.

"Miss Cassie." Sam rolled my name around on his tongue to see if it fit.

"Miss Cassie works at a school," Luke continued.

I barely had time to be surprised that Luke knew how I made my living or to process the fact that my aunt had given Luke my vital statistics after all because Sam chose that moment to let out a squeal. I studied the boy more closely. He had a starstruck look in his eyes.

"Are you a real teacher? Like at preschool? I go to preschool. I'm four."

He appeared so in awe of me that I didn't want to burst his bubble. Why was it that little ones always assumed only teachers worked at schools instead of administrators, paraprofessionals and other support staff?

"No, I'm not a teacher, but I still work with a lot of children. I'm a speech pathologist."

"Oh." He nodded, my answer seeming to satisfy him, but since he started playing with his handheld video game, I took it my hero-admiration session had ended.

Without Sam's constant chattering, the air in the truck cab grew stuffier than if Luke had been blasting heat instead of the air-conditioning. I'd always wondered if someone could die from social discomfort, and I figured I was about to have my answer.

"Aunt Eleanor sure looks beautiful tonight," I said

when any inane comment seemed better than letting this silence linger.

Luke made one of those grunting sounds that men like to use instead of words. Only real words count as far as I'm concerned, but I continued anyway, as if he'd spoken, tried to make eye contact and made a real effort.

"I think it's great that my aunt and your mother have been friends for as long as they have. How many of us can say we have friends like that?"

"Not many." He didn't look at me as he followed the line of cars down the winding, tree-lined road that led to town. Though he didn't mention whether he had any friends like that, if he was the sweetheart with other people that he'd been to me, I was guessing no. Maybe he'd never heard the whole catching-more-flies-with-honey argument.

I tried again though I didn't know why I was making the effort. Talking to Luke Sheridan was like trying to break through a brick wall with conversation when only a sledgehammer would do the job.

"I'm so happy for my aunt and uncle. Twenty-five years of marriage is a major accomplishment these days."

Luke slowed to a stop at one of Mantua's few traffic lights, and he turned to face me, his expression tight. "Look, I'm sure you're a nice person, but—" He cleared his throat and started again. "I don't know what my mother told you when she said she would set you up, but she was wrong."

"Told me?" Even I heard the squeak in my voice, so I didn't kid myself into believing he didn't hear it. "You think I would have subjected myself to this humiliation *on purpose?*"

Clearly he had or he wouldn't have been looking at me with an expression every bit as incredulous as the one I had trained on him. "You mean you didn't know—"

"No!"

I jerked at the harsh sound of my own voice, and looked up to see the light change. I waited for him to pass through the intersection and sneaked a peek back at Sam, who was still mesmerized by his game, before I continued.

"I've been avoiding matchmakers like a good case of malaria ever since the—well, for a while now."

My cheeks burned, and I stared at my hands in my lap. I couldn't believe I'd almost mentioned the divorce out loud when I'd become an expert at pretending it hadn't happened. All is well on the banks of *denial*, after all.

"Kind of hard to escape this particular Cupid, huh?"

My head came up with a snap. Had the sourpuss just made a joke? "Aunt Eleanor? Probably would have been a little awkward, I'll give you that. But I would have found some excuse if I'd known what my aunt had planned."

"Like you had to wash your hair?"

"And do deep conditioning, of course."

"Of course." He shrugged. "I just wish I could have avoided this overromanticized tribute to matrimonial bliss altogether."

"Now don't hold back, Luke. Tell me what you really think." I couldn't help chuckling, as the tension between us eased. "Wait. I'm related to the bride. I had to be here. What's your excuse?"

"You don't know my mom very well, do you?"

"What do you mean?"

"She's a transplanted Southern belle, and she's used to getting her way." He jerked the hand that wasn't on the steering wheel toward me as if to toss out his earlier comment. "What can I say? I'm a mama's boy to the core."

I grinned at his profile, surprised and pleased that he would admit that. He shook his head, clearly as startled as I was by what he'd said, but then he glanced sidelong at me and smiled, a tiny dimple appearing on his right cheek.

I tried not to notice, really I did. Just a single cute dimple and a smile in my direction, and I was feeling tingly inside all the way to my bare toes in my strappy sandals. That was just pitiful.

And as quickly as that, the tension that had dissipated inside the truck cab was back and doing a pretty good job of stealing all the oxygen. If I were in the habit of being honest with myself, I might have admitted that this tension was different than the other—about awareness rather than avoidance—but why go and change my habits when they were working for me?

The silence seemed louder this time, our chorused breathing and the air conditioner's drone the only interruptions as we pulled into the parking lot of Gino's Taste of Italy. Was Luke waiting for me to say something? If so, what did he expect me to say? And what if I didn't want to be the one to speak up first? I sat for several long seconds, waiting him to give in and fill the silence.

Say something, will you.

Somebody spoke up, all right. It just wasn't who I expected.

"Daddy, what's a matchmaker?"

Chapter Three

I glanced down the long line of checkered-cloth covered tables that had been pushed together at Gino's. Far too many of us were crammed into spots along those tables, but nobody seemed to mind. In fact, from the laughter coming from various spots throughout the room, everyone seemed to be having a wonderful time.

Except Luke, the grouch.

Sitting across the table from me, a few people down, he'd been quiet all through dinner, had barely touched his baked ziti. Every time I'd caught his eye, he'd scowled at me. Okay, I had to admit that he might have had a small reason to be annoyed. A forty-pound reason.

I couldn't help it that most of the seats were already taken when we'd arrived at the restaurant or that when there were two remaining side-by-side seats that Sam had begged to sit by me instead of his dad. With Luke's sour expression, who would blame his son for making that choice?

"Hey, Miss Cassie, look. I have a mustache."

Sam looked up from his sundae to show me his upper lip, which he had now painted with chocolate fudge. While the rest of the adults were still finishing their entrées, the child had already moved on to dessert.

"Wow, that's a pretty fancy job you've done there."

"It's chocolate."

"No way. I thought it was a real mustache."

I didn't mention the chocolate that had made its way down to Sam's pale yellow polo shirt and had combined with the remnants of garlic bread and marinara sauce already there. Glancing at Luke, I caught him frowning at me again. I shouldn't have been encouraging Sam's mischievousness, but he was just so adorable that I couldn't resist.

Sam reached a grubby hand over to twirl his finger in one of the tendrils at my cheek. I could just imagine how stiff my hair would be when he was finished with it, but the sweet gesture made me smile. That same dull ache I'd felt earlier when he'd crawled into my lap and hugged me, settled in my chest, making me wish for things that might have been.

To avoid the pain that came with wishing, I tucked the thought away as I looked up from the last of my fettuccini Alfredo. From across the table, I felt as much as saw Luke's gaze on us, intense and not quite pleased. I wished my cheeks didn't have to burn like that, letting everyone know what I was thinking.

Luke blinked a few times and turned his head to look at the other end of the table, but I sensed that I'd seen something raw, something unmasked in him, before he'd shuttered it away. I stared at my plate again, stirring my fork in the remaining sauce.

"One of the Sheridan men sure has hit it off with the flower girl," the handsome older gentleman who'd introduced himself as Marcus Sheridan said from across the table.

Sitting next to him, Luke elbowed his father. "Cut it out, Dad."

Marcus only laughed. "Sam sure has a thing for blondes, and this one isn't too hard on the eyes, either. But I'm sure you hadn't noticed."

Luke narrowed his gaze at his father but didn't answer.

"I know somebody who shouldn't be paying attention to such things at his age." Yvonne Sheridan leaned forward from where she was seated on Marcus's other side and waved a warning finger at him.

"My eyes haven't given out on me yet."

That little comment earned him another elbow—this time from his wife. Even Luke fought back a smile.

The boy sitting next to me appeared oblivious to the conversation as he sat stirring the rest of his sundae into chocolate soup.

I turned back to Luke. "Do you want me to clean him up? You'll never get those stains out of that shirt."

"No, I've got it." He paused, straightening in his seat. "And you'd be amazed at the stains I can get out of clothes."

With that, he picked up a small canvas bag I hadn't noticed him carrying into the restaurant and came around the table to his son.

"Okay, buddy, it's time."

Instead of asking "for what?" as I was tempted to, Sam popped down from his seat and followed his dad into the men's room. When the pair reemerged minutes later, the boy's face was scrubbed clean, and he was dressed in an identical polo shirt to the stained one he'd been wearing before. Even his hair had been combed into place.

Sam pulled away from his dad and climbed back into the chair next to me. He scrunched his face into a nasty look. "My hair looks stupid."

"You look great." I brushed my fingers through his damp hair and looked up at his father. "What an amazing transformation."

"Not amazing," Luke answered, though he was clearly pleased that I thought so. "We're just prepared." He held up the canvas bag, where he must have put the soiled shirt.

Marcus waved a hand in Luke's direction as Luke returned to his seat. "Our son took the Boy Scout motto, 'Be Prepared,' to heart when it comes to parenting. Always ready with wet wipes and extra clothes. Probably has a kitchen sink somewhere in that bag."

At his father's challenge, Luke took a peek inside it. "Nope. But there are bandages, antibiotic ointment, liquid antihistamine and meat tenderizer." He must have seen my confused expression because he added, "The last two are for bee stings."

"As I said, always prepared." Marcus's deep laughter filled the room.

When I looked up again, I found Luke watching me,

his gaze lingering. I should have turned away—I knew that—but I felt pinned under the intensity of his study.

At the reverberating *thunk* of a portable microphone, I jerked the way I used to when my mother caught me sneaking snacks before dinner. Looking away from Luke, I glanced guiltily at his parents, but their attention was on the portly, white-haired man who stood with the microphone in his hand.

"Hi, everyone. I'm Tom Wilder, the best man for this little shindig—last time and this one. I don't know why, but this guy wanted me back again." He paused to pat Jack Hudson on the shoulder.

"If there's a third time, I might want to get that young Orlando Bloom to play my role since he looks a lot more like the original than this snow-topped version."

The best man got the laugh he was going for, but I had a hard time picturing the old Santa Claus character as ever looking like any of Hollywood's leading men. The smile pulling on Luke's lips suggested he had a similar theory.

"Are you sure you don't mean Andy Rooney?" Marcus called out, earning his own round of laughter.

"Hey, stem the chatter from the peanut gallery," Jack called out but in a genial tone.

Marcus raised both hands in apology, still chuckling.

Tom cleared his throat and started again. "I'm sure we'll have plenty of time for this tomorrow, but I wanted to be the first to toast to the *still*-happy couple."

My uncle wrapped his arm around his bride. "We've got a lot to be happy about, old friend."

"Well, are you going to let me finish this or not?" Tom asked him.

Jack waved a hand to tell him to continue.

"Thanks." Tom shook his head as he gripped his glass of iced tea. "As I was saying—again—I wanted to offer a toast. So let's lift our glasses to honor our friends Jack and Eleanor."

"To Jack and Eleanor" came a chorus of voices, followed by an instrumental selection provided by the clinking of iced tea and lemonade glasses along with porcelain coffee cups. Following a round of applause, Eleanor stepped forward and offered directions for the next day's ceremony.

Sam leaned close to me and did his four-year-old imitation of a whisper, which really was just a shout cupped between two little hands. "Do you get to go to the wedding tomorrow?"

I nodded but pressed a finger to my lips, trying to hush him.

"It's going to be on the beach."

Pulling Sam into my lap, I cuddled him and spoke in a whisper much quieter than his. "I know. It will be fun."

My own words surprised me. It was first time I'd thought anything remotely positive about this weekend's event. Agony. Misery. Now those were words I had associated with my participation in my aunt and uncle's vows renewal ceremony. But fun?

I shrugged. Maybe it would be. Sam would be there, after all, and that little boy had enough energy to entertain us all day long. But I had the idea that part of my budding excitement about tomorrow's events had to do with having another chance to see the little boy's father.

* * *

I frowned as I smoothed my hands down the filmy overskirt of my pale yellow bridesmaid's dress and paced along the wall of windows where my aunt's house spread itself open for a landscape view of Lake Michigan. Mine was a bridesmaid's gown rather than a flower girl's dress because formal-wear designers never planned on almost-thirty-year-old flower girls. Hoped against them, I would guess.

As I lowered my gaze to the oversize basket of daisies my family members expected me to carry, I decided that the dressmakers had a good reason for committing age discrimination. A grown woman probably looked like a baby elephant while sprinkling flowers in the bride's path.

"Oh good, you're still here," Aunt Eleanor said as she walked up behind me. "Have you seen Princess around? I haven't seen her all morning."

"Um, I saw her with Uncle Jack earlier." I didn't mention that he'd been *this* close to having to pry the cat's talons out of my leg when my only crime was to sneak past to get a cup of coffee in the kitchen. Okay, maybe the furry monster's claw attack was really only a threatening crouch and spit, but you get the picture.

"I should go look for her. She's probably hungry and thirsty. Maybe she got out and—"

I shook my head to interrupt her. "I'm sure she's fine. Uncle Jack told me he was going to feed her. Now she's probably full and happily napping under a bed." I could only hope it wasn't mine.

"She could be hiding, too. She hates crowds."

And everything else from what I could tell, but I only said, "That's probably it. We'll track her down right after the ceremony, but you need to get ready."

"I suppose you're right."

My aunt looked regal in white layers of cascading lace that fell to a tea-length hemline. She wore no veil, instead had pulled back her hair, with baby's breath woven into tiny braids at her temples. She turned her back so I could finish closing her zipper.

"You make a beautiful bride." I wrapped my arms around her middle from behind and squeezed, careful to avoid getting makeup on her dress. "So you chose white?" I tried and failed to keep my voice level as I asked that one.

Eleanor answered with a girlish giggle. "Now I don't want any Miss Manners comments about which brides should be wearing white. I wore an ivory gown the first time, so I wanted to try something different. Besides I didn't want to wear a cream-colored dress and match the sand."

"Wouldn't want you to disappear on your wedding day."

"Exactly. You look pretty wonderful yourself today."

"That's thanks to you for not choosing periwinkle again."

Eleanor stepped to the huge mirror on the great room wall to check her makeup. "Better thank Yvonne for that. She told me if I picked that color again I would have to find another matron of honor."

Outside, crowd members were beginning to take their seats on white folding chairs lined in rows in the sand. A few of the groomsmen milled about in tuxedos, seating guests, but the particular tuxedo-clad guest I was looking for was nowhere to be seen.

"Do I thank Yvonne for getting to go barefoot, as well?" I lifted the hem of my own tea-length dress and curled my bare, pale-painted toes in the carpet.

"Nope. That was my Jack's idea. He suggested the wedding on the beach and the barefoot plan."

I lowered my hem. "Remind me to kiss him later."

"As long as I get to kiss him first." Eleanor patted her hair once more while examining her image in the mirror. "Let's go. I'm ready to get this thing started."

As we exited through the side door, I resisted the urge to reach up and pat my hair that I had curled and then left loose for the occasion. It shouldn't have mattered what Luke thought about my appearance, but I wouldn't waste time trying to convince myself that it didn't.

In fact, just the thought of him had that same nervous tension flowing through me that I'd felt every time I'd caught him watching me last night. It was an embarrassing reaction, I realized, since he was probably only watching me to keep an eye on his son. I didn't know what it said about me that I was getting keyed up when Luke wasn't even around, but the word *pathetic* did come to mind.

I straightened my shoulders and pushed my unproductive thoughts aside as we descended the stairs to the lower deck where a few of the bridesmaids and groomsmen had gathered.

"There you are," Yvonne said, stepping forward to hug her best friend. "Jack was worried you were standing him up at the altar."

"Not on his life," Eleanor said with a hearty laugh. "He's not going to get rid of me yet."

"Do we have everyone now?" Yvonne asked, taking control of the situation in her role as matron of honor.

We all turned to glance at the makeshift bridal chapel, with its rows of chairs, simple lectern and floral arrangements and speakers on platforms. Sam was standing in one of the chairs and waving madly at me until his grandpa wrangled him back into his seat.

Order was temporary at best as the youngster flipped around in his chair, sticking his legs through the hole in the back. I waved at him and mouthed a hello, but the little flirt one-upped me by blowing me a kiss.

Careful not get lipstick on my hand that would wind up on my dress, I touched my fingers to my mouth and tossed out an elaborately blown kiss. What I hadn't expected, though, was that someone would step between my original target and me.

Luke. It took me several seconds before I even remembered to lower the hand that hung suspended next to my face.

He recovered more quickly than I did, smiling as he trod through the sand toward the rest of the wedding party.

From the pictures, I knew he'd been a cute kid in a tuxedo all those years ago, but the man wearing the white tuxedo jacket and black bow tie and cummerbund this time was a cross between a fairy-tale prince and a hunky beach volleyball player. Even his bare feet beneath his black trousers just made it appear as if he was going for casual chic.

"Happy wedding day, everyone." He took the time

to exchange greetings with each member of the wedding party. When he finally reached me, he winked.

"Well, don't you look like a sunny day in that dress," he said when he stepped closer to me.

His gaze settled on my hair that at the moment was already streaming across my face. I tucked it behind my ear. Maybe wearing it loose hadn't been such a good idea after all.

"You probably say that to all the girls you're partnered with in a wedding party."

Luke drew his eyebrows together and appeared to ponder my comment before he answered. "Yes, I believe I've said that to *every* woman who's been my partner in a wedding."

"Been in a lot of weddings, have you?" I just couldn't help carrying the joke a bit further.

"Just two, and in the other one, they paired me with the bride."

"Oh," I said as the joke fell flat. I was tempted to allow dated images of myself as an ill-fated bride to invade the moment, but with effort, I shut down Memory Lane.

Luke's gaze was on me when I rejoined the moment, and his knowing expression told me he had an idea where I'd traveled during my mental intermission.

"How about we don't go there today?" he said. "How about we try to have as much fun as Jack and Eleanor will this afternoon and save the bittersweet memories for another time?"

My relief came out as an audible sigh that made him grin again. "Sounds like a great idea to me."

Yvonne pressed between us then, looking back and forth and wearing a strange expression. "Hey, you two, there'll be plenty of time for socializing later. Right now we need to get this wedding over with, so get in line."

Luke put his arm around his mother's shoulder. "Okay, Mom, but don't you want to check first to see if I need to use the little boys' room?"

She tilted her head so she could look up at him and lifted an eyebrow. "Well…do you?"

"Uh, no," he said, clearing his throat. "I'm good."

Yvonne blew out an exasperated breath and turned to me in a conspiratorial pose. "Children. They never *really* grow up."

"Not if we can help it," Luke quipped. Again he winked at me, and this time I grinned.

The sound operator picked this moment to cue up "The Wedding March," so I joined Luke and the three bridesmaids as we arranged ourselves for our march down the sandy aisle. I wouldn't have to worry about doing that silly step-together-step bridal march thing. All I had to do was manage to get down the aisle without falling over in the sand, and all would be well.

Arriving from the north side of the house, an anxious-looking Uncle Jack and his groomsmen took their places on the right side of the lectern.

This wasn't a real wedding—we all knew that—but the fact that it wasn't only made Jack's nervousness that much more endearing. He looked the part of the terrified groom, excited by the prospect of a future with this woman and yet convinced that it was all too good to be true.

Suddenly I felt ashamed I'd ever been reluctant to participate in this event. Jack and Eleanor had an amazing relationship, and I couldn't help feeling privileged to be a part of celebrating their continuing love story.

I watched as each of the bridesmaids proceeded down the aisle, reiterating the statement of friendship they'd made for my aunt and uncle twenty-five years before. Luke was next, a tall and proud representation of the continuing bond between his mother and my aunt as lifelong friends.

And then it was my turn. With a pride that I never could have understood as a child, I made my own barefoot march down the sandy aisle, paving the way for the bride with a trail of daisies. I felt none of the pain I had expected over my own scars, but only joy over a marriage that had already beat the odds and held nothing but promise for the future.

Once I took my place near the floral arrangement and the silver-haired minister invited the crowd to stand, I turned to see Aunt Eleanor making her entrance. Though there were lines on her face and more softness about her hips than the first time she made this journey, love shone in her eyes, as I'm sure it had the first time. Her gaze remained on her groom alone with each step she took.

My heart squeezed, and my eyes burned as these images shimmered in front of me. Though I'd always frowned on women who cried at weddings, right now I didn't care. This was how love was supposed to be. This was what God intended when He created marriage.

Would I ever know love like my aunt and uncle had experienced? No, I couldn't allow myself to worry about that now. No matter what the future held for me, just having the opportunity to witness love like this gave me hope.

Chapter Four

By the time the tour bus rolled to a stop again in front of my relatives' home, the lake was swallowing one of those much-anticipated, burnished-orange sunsets, and I felt as if I'd run a marathon—in heels.

Once I had my feet on solid ground again, I slipped out of the offending strappy sandals. I couldn't hold the shoes solely to blame for my weary body, though, since I'd only worn them during the dinner and mingling portion of the evening. Apparently, at the Mantua Yacht Club the no shirt, no shoes, no service rule applied even for receptions following barefoot weddings.

"Bet you can't catch me." Sam snatched one of the shoes that had been dangling from my fingers and took off toward the house.

I could only watch him listlessly, my impetus to get up and go already gotten up and gone. "I bet you're right," I called after him.

"Just one day, and the kid already wore you out?"

I didn't need the tingling on the back of my neck to

tell me who'd come off the bus behind me. His light musky cologne drifted over my shoulder as the breeze tickled my ear. Bending my neck and rubbing my ear against my shoulder, I answered without looking back.

"It's been a long day. That's all."

"Long but surprisingly fun, wasn't it?"

At first, I made an affirmative sound in my throat, but then remembering how little I appreciated Luke's nonanswers, I turned to him just as he caught up with me. Luke appeared far more comfortable now that he'd removed his bow tie and rolled up his sleeves, his tuxedo jacket draped over his arm.

"Yeah, it was fun." More fun than I'd had any right to ask for, especially considering how I'd dreaded the event.

"Whenever you got a breather from being chased by my son, you mean?"

"No, the whole day was great. Partly because of your son." And partly because of his father, but I didn't figure it would be wise to add that. We would just end up back at square one, where Luke was convinced I had something to do with my aunt's and his mother's matchmaking scheme. Still, whether I admitted it or not, I'd laughed more today when Luke was the one telling the jokes.

"Which part did you like best, when he spilled the whole bottle of steak sauce on his plate or when he smeared wedding cake on my face?"

The memory of Luke with globs of white buttercream frosting in his sideburns, like a premature case of especially tasty gray hair, brought a smile to my lips.

Luke glanced sidelong at me. "Don't answer that."

His hand moved to the neatly trimmed line of hair in front of his ear. It had to be stiff by now.

"Come on, Luke. Sam was adorable today."

"Adorable. Right. No wonder some animals eat their young."

Okay, maybe he'd been a little naughty, but nothing to warrant being served up with barbecue sauce, in my opinion. In fact, Sam's single-minded pursuit of my attention, from squeezing in next to me in the buffet line to saving me a seat by him on the bus, had been downright endearing. He was as sweet and eager to please as a child of my own might have been.

"What's that secret smile about? What are you not saying?"

My posture and my expression tightened over being caught daydreaming impossibilities again.

"I wasn't trying to get you to stop smiling. Only asking what made you smile."

I shrugged but didn't look at him. "He's a great kid is all," I said, opting for a blanket truth if I couldn't be more specific. "This place is beautiful at night. I heard you don't live too far from here. You probably spend a lot of time at the beach."

"Not much. My job keeps me busy."

He didn't mention that his son kept him hopping, too, but I wouldn't have expected any less from Sam.

"Aunt Eleanor said you work for a real estate developer?"

"I'm pretty much Clyde Lewis's hands and feet. Clyde is loaded, so he likes to write the checks, and I handle all the rest. The permits, the subcontractors, the headaches. We've worked together ten years, and we've tripled company holdings since then."

I couldn't help being impressed. There was just something about a man with drive that got to me every time.

I would have asked him more—I knew how much men liked to talk about themselves—but he surprised me by turning the subject back to me.

"So what does a speech pathologist do? Your aunt tried to explain it, but I didn't really get it."

He also probably wasn't listening too closely when Aunt Eleanor was marketing me like an infomercial, but I kept that to myself.

"Speech paths—that's what we call ourselves—identify and diagnose speech and language disorders."

"You mean like stuttering?"

"That's one," I said. "Stuttering is a fluency disorder, but I also work with children who have articulation disorders, meaning difficulty pronouncing certain sounds.

"Really, most of my caseload are students who have trouble learning language and semantics and have trouble learning grammar functions. Besides working with groups of students, I do initial screenings and in-depth evaluations with other professionals such as the school psychologist and an occupational therapist."

"Sounds like challenging work."

I stopped walking and turned to study him, certain he was making fun of me. He was looking back at me, but he wasn't smiling. "Sorry about that. I do go on sometimes."

"I did ask. Anyway, you seem to love your job."

"I do. I like seeing the kids showing improvement in functional ways. It makes their lives better."

"Your students are lucky to have you."

My skin warmed with pleasure. "Thanks." A gal could get used to hearing praise like that. I wondered if he would mind hanging around the hallways at my school to offer encouragement whenever I was having a tough day.

"Looks like you got a sunburn today," he said, moving on to another subject.

"I did. Just my face and shoulders. I never thought to wear sunscreen to a wedding."

"You mean it wasn't on your list. Dress, basket of flowers, sunscreen."

"I'll put it on my list next time."

"Next time?" His baritone laughter drifted on the breeze. "I sure hope these two lovebirds don't try this thing again in another twenty-five years. I'll be the first gray-haired ring bearer ever."

"And I'll look like a mess as a fifty-four-year-old flower girl."

I wasn't certain, but I thought I heard him say, "I doubt that."

But when he looked back at me again, he lifted an eyebrow. "Fifty-four? Don't you mean fifty-five?"

I shook my head. "You might be thirty, but one of us is still twenty-nine. I doubt you'll remember this, but I was only four when I was my aunt's flower girl."

A slow smile spread across Luke's lips. "So I take it there are months until your milestone thirtieth birthday?"

"It's a month from today—the third of July."

"You were an early firecracker baby?"

"Something like that."

As soon as we rounded the house, the crisp breeze off the lake enveloped me, snaking over my sunburned shoulders and between my shoulder blades. I shivered. The filmy material of my dress just wouldn't do now that the last sunlight had disappeared.

"Here." Luke draped his jacket around my shoulders.

"Thanks." Pulling the jacket more tightly around me, I shrugged off the tingling at my shoulders where his fingers had brushed. I just hadn't warmed up yet.

We paused when we reached the landing at the top of the drive. Up ahead of us, Sam had crossed over the deck and was tripping down the weather-roughened wood stairs that led to the beach.

Luke gestured with a nod of his head toward his son. "I'd better catch him. He probably won't toss your shoe into the lake, but you never know what a boy will do when the adrenaline gets going."

"You don't think he'll throw *himself* into the lake, do you?"

His only answer was a nervous shrug before we both hurried across the deck and down the same stairs the boy had taken.

"Sam, stop!"

Luke might as well have yelled into a spinning fan—the wind and the crash of waves easily muffled his command. Without bothering to take off his shoes, Sam plowed out onto the beach, past the site where the wedding had taken place. He seemed to be running straight toward the dark expanse of water.

Luke shot out across the beach, calling out to his son again. This time Sam stopped and turned around. His shoulders hunched, he stomped back to us.

Still holding my shoe, Sam frowned up at me. "You were supposed to chase me."

"And you're not *supposed* to get in the water by yourself," Luke answered before I could say anything.

"I wasn't in the water." Sam drew his eyebrows together, looking at his father as if he thought Luke was missing a few volumes of his encyclopedia set.

Luke grunted, and I managed to squelch a laugh. The kid did have a point. His shoes were sandy but not wet.

"True," Luke said finally. "You're not supposed to run off with people's things, either."

Sam looked down at the shoe in his hand and then up at me. "Uh…sorry."

He slipped the strap of the shoe back over my fingers alongside its mate.

"No damage done." Reaching down with my free hand, I brushed back his windblown hair. "Sorry, I was too tired to play chase right now."

The incident immediately forgotten, Sam turned back to Luke. "On the bus, Mrs. Hudson said we're going to eat some more wedding cake."

"Look, Sam, I'm sure she didn't mean us." He took his son's hand and led him to the deck steps. "She was probably talking about—"

"No, Daddy. She did. She really did. She meant us. Please, can we stay?"

Instead of answering, Luke half led, half dragged

Sam up the steps. The boy was doing an award-worthy performance of a rag doll, while I followed gamely behind.

"Of course, you'll stay." The words came from above us.

The voice turned out to be my aunt's. She was looking down from the deck, already alight with miniature strands and huge floods. Aunt Eleanor looked comfortable now, having traded her white gown for a pink velour sweat suit. Only the flowers still woven in her hair hinted she had so recently been a bride.

Luke hoisted Sam up on his hip to climb the last few steps. "Sorry, Eleanor. It's late, and I need to get Sam to bed."

"Everybody's got time for one more piece of cake."

"No, really—"

Having reached the landing beside them, I shook my head to interrupt his argument. "You're wasting your breath. My aunt's power of persuasion is just as legendary as your mom's, and you know how well that went."

Luke's jaw tightened, but he raised his hands in surrender. "Fine. One piece. Then it's home to bed."

Eleanor brushed her hand across her brow in an exaggerated gesture. "Whew. I thought that was going to be a tough argument."

I would have agreed with her, and it was unsettling how pleased I felt that Luke and Sam would be staying a while longer. Mostly Sam. It had to be about Sam, right?

"Yea!" Sam called, the rag doll quickly replaced by an animated little boy.

My uncle pulled open the sliding-glass door. "Either get inside and get a piece of this cake or I'll have to eat more. Wouldn't want any of it to go to waste."

"How good of you to think with a conservationist's mind, dear."

Everyone laughed at Eleanor's comment except for Sam, who was too busy scrambling out of his father's arms and rushing into the house to notice.

Eleanor watched him go before turning back to Luke and me. "You didn't have to tell him twice."

Luke just shook his head. "Now there's a boy who needs more sugar tonight."

Still, Luke couldn't hide his look of amusement and adoration as he watched his son through the window. That expression of a proud father couldn't be faked. My heart squeezed for more reasons than I wanted to analyze.

When my aunt cleared her throat, I realized I wasn't the only one who'd been watching Luke, or me for that matter. She glanced back and forth between us, her eyes widening as she took in the fact that I was still wearing Luke's jacket.

I was tempted to shed it right then, but that would have only have made it seem like a big deal that he'd let me wear it. And it wasn't a big deal—just a gentlemanly gesture and that was all.

"Well, we'd better get some cake before my Jack makes good on his threat to eat it all." Eleanor yawned behind her hand. "I do believe I'm about to wilt, and I still have to show my niece here Princess's routine so we can leave on our honeymoon tomorrow."

Eleanor crossed the deck and stepped through the slider, closing the screen door behind her. Air-conditioning wasn't usually necessary at night because of the breeze off the water, but with the bugs, screens were always a must.

Once she was gone, Luke turned back to me, his eyebrow raised.

"I'm cat-sitting and house-sitting." I supplied the answer as if it were the smallest thing in the world. Taking care of Princess would be anything but a small undertaking.

"For how long?"

"Three weeks. Just until my aunt and uncle get back from Europe."

He glanced over his shoulder at the amazing house and then turned back to me. "How'd you end up pulling tough duty like that?"

"Family connections. What can I say?"

Starting into the house, I turned and motioned for Luke to follow. I set my shoes on the floor next to the door and slipped off Luke's tuxedo jacket, pressing it into his arms.

"Thanks. I appreciate it." I rubbed my hands together, trying to ignore the odd sensation in my fingers from having brushed his.

My aunt was already in the kitchen dishing up slices from the remaining hunk of wedding cake. Several other guests, most of whom had already traded their wedding attire for casual comfort, were scattered about the great room, chatting or nibbling on leftovers. Uncle Jack and Sam sat at the bar that divided the great room from the kitchen, eating pieces of cake and drinking from tall glasses of milk.

I sauntered past them barefoot into the kitchen and lifted the cake server from Eleanor's hand. I sliced a few more pieces and placed them on the clear glass dessert plates my aunt had spread out on the counter.

"You're tired," I told her. "You don't have to show me everything tonight. Just make a list. I'll be able to figure it out." If I couldn't manage something as simple as a list of cat duties, then my master's degree wasn't worth the parchment it was written on.

"We won't have much time before church, and we have to leave for the Muskegon Airport right after," Jack pointed out. "You know, it's rush-rush-rush so we can fly to Detroit Metro for that long layover. What is it, four hours?"

Eleanor nodded. "I guess if we hurry in the morning, we'll be able to show you everything. Our sweetie will need her three meals plus snacks."

As she spoke, she ticked off list items on her fingers. "Her litter box will need regular scooping and fully changing every third day. Then there's playtime with her toys and, of course, her drinks."

"Drinks?" Luke and I both asked at the same time, and I glanced back at him, surprised to find him behind me. He reached past me to take one of the plates, a fork and a napkin.

Uncle Jack's rumble of laughter filled the room. "It's a funny story, isn't it, Ellie?"

"It's funny, all right." She gave her husband a warm look before letting the rest of the crowd in on the joke. "When Princess was a kitten, we used to turn the faucet on to let her bat at the water. Cats like to do that sometimes. Well, as it turns out, she likes to drink from the faucet, too."

"But she also drinks from a water bowl, right?" Luke asked.

Eleanor shook her head. "No, not really. I mean she might if every faucet in the house were broken and there wasn't a flowing drop to spare, but I've never seen evidence that she even touches her water bowl."

"And my tenderhearted Ellie thought it would be cruel to dehydrate the little tooters just to break her of the habit when we were always around anyway." Jack explained.

"Princess is a little...privileged then?" Luke said.

"Spoiled rotten is what she is," Jack said, laughing again. "She rules the roost around here, but we love her anyway."

"She's our baby," Eleanor agreed.

Everybody seemed to think this was hilarious—everyone except me. I was too busy trying to fight off the cloud of doom dangling over me. What had I gotten myself into? Princess turned into a feline chainsaw whenever we crossed paths, and I was expected to give her drinks from the faucet. I would have to feed her and play with her and make sure her kitty potty smelled fresh all while having to avoid the business end of her claws.

While the others continued to laugh, Luke leaned close to me and whispered, "It's not such a plum job after all."

I shrugged since he had a point.

Yvonne and Marcus Sheridan, who'd been talking to some other guests in the great room, made their way into the kitchen together, and Yvonne rested an elbow on the bar next to her grandson.

"It looks as if we've done justice to the cake." Yvonne turned to admire the platter where only crumbs and a thick wedge of decorator icing remained to suggest there'd once been a three-tiered cake.

"It's all gone," Sam observed, swiping his finger across the platter and popping the frosting in his mouth.

Luke shook his head, probably to discourage his son from double-dipping. "Yes, it is, and it's also time for us to go."

"But, Daddy."

But, Luke. I had to look around to determine whether I'd said it out loud. *Why* I'd almost said it was a whole other matter. A dozen or so wedding guests remained in my aunt and uncle's great room, so it wasn't as if I'd be alone when they left, but I sensed that most of the fun I'd been having all night would leave with Luke and his son.

"But nothing," Luke told him. "We're out of here." He lifted his son and spun around until the boy giggled.

When Luke set him on his feet again, Sam turned to me, holding his arms wide to steady himself. "Grammy said you're staying here for three whole weeks."

"I am. It'll be nice to relax."

"Grammy said when your aunt and uncle leave that you'll be lonely."

"Oh, she did, did she?" Luke glared at his mother, who only smiled back at him.

Apparently, Yvonne hadn't given up on her match-making scheme, and from the silly expression on my aunt's face, I guessed she wasn't willing to throw in the towel, either. I should have been mad enough to throw a towel—or something with better aim—at the both of them, but I wasn't. I didn't even want to think about what that might mean.

"Me and Daddy can come over tomorrow so you won't be lonely. We could go swimming at the beach and make sand castles and—"

"Samuel—"

"Wow," I said, interrupting another one of Luke's parental warning growls. "That's so nice of you to think of me."

His gaze focused on me instead of his father, Sam beamed.

"You know better than to invite yourself over to people's houses," Luke said.

That sweet smile fell, and I found myself grasping for a way to put it back on Sam's little face. A bribe of more cake came to mind, but there weren't enough crumbs on that platter to satisfy a mouse with a sweet tooth.

"Hey, that's all right," I said.

"No…it's not."

Luke's words and his tight expression didn't leave room for argument, especially since he was right. I shouldn't have been sticking my nose in when Luke was trying to teach his son good manners. Sam had no business inviting himself over to my house—well, for the next three weeks it was my house, anyway.

"Sorry, Miss Cassie."

"I forgive you."

"That's better." Luke bent slightly so he could rest his hand on his son's shoulder.

As I looked between father and son, I couldn't help smiling. Just because Sam wasn't allowed to invite himself places didn't mean the boy and his father couldn't accept an invitation from me. And I realized with a start that I wanted badly to ask.

There were so many reasons why I should resist the impulse, not the least of which was the baggage I carried inside me, and if mine wasn't enough, Luke probably had a suitcase or a duffel bag to spare.

What was I thinking? Sam had only suggested a day at the beach, not a lifetime commitment. My brain had to be on wedding overload today. Too much wedding music. Too much lace and chiffon. Even too much of that heady scent of flowers. Wedding lag. That and a sunburn, too. And I'd thought I was a real mess before I showed up in Mantua.

Luke hefted Sam up on his hip and turned to his mother. "We'll see you tomorrow at church."

Yvonne stepped to them, reaching up to kiss her son and grandson.

"I need some sugar, too." Eleanor shuffled over for her own round of kisses.

"Thanks for everything," Luke said when he extracted himself from her embrace. With four long strides, he was standing at the door. It must have been as an afterthought that he turned back to face me and waved.

"Hey, Luke, Sam, wait up."

My outburst surprised me as much as it had Luke.

As nonchalantly as a woman could after she'd just hollered across the room, I made my way over to them. I avoided eye contact with any of the other adults, though I could sense their gazes on me.

"What's up?" Luke asked when I stood in front of them.

"I would like to invite you and Sam to come over tomorrow afternoon for a day at the beach."

Luke was already shaking his head before I finished. "Cassie, I already said Sam couldn't come over."

"No, you said he couldn't invite himself here."

"That's not—" He stopped himself, seeming to think for a minute before he gave an exaggerated shrug. He couldn't argue that I had a point.

"Well?" I pressed while I had an advantage.

I could just imagine the parental wheels turning in Luke's head. Should he give in? Was it really giving in to Sam's begging when they now had a proper invitation? Would it establish a precedent that if Sam begged long enough at those candy traps in the grocery store checkout lanes that his father would fold?

"Please, Daddy. Can we?"

For several seconds, Luke said nothing, but when he did, he spoke to his son instead of me. "I think a day at the beach would be okay, particularly since we were invited." Once he'd made that point, he glanced back at me. "That'd be great. Thanks for asking."

I nodded, trying to appear only moderately pleased.

"Are we skipping church?" Sam asked.

"Of course not. We'll come *after* church."

"But Daddy—"

"No buts about it."

Sam opened his mouth to protest, but seeing the firm set of his father's jaw, shut it again. I wasn't sure why it impressed me so much that church was nonnegotiable at Luke's house, especially when I'd declined my aunt's invitation to join her and my uncle at services in the morning. Maybe it just comforted me to know someone was where I needed to be.

It had taken them nearly a half hour, but Luke and Sam finally went out the door. I made a point of not staring after them as I sensed I was still being watched. Instead, I busied myself clearing away dessert plates and dishes. I loaded the dishwasher, at first trying my best to keep from smiling, and then, finding little success, at least keeping my back to any prying eyes.

None of those eyes would be around tomorrow. I should have been relieved to finally escape the microscope—really this time—but I couldn't help feeling keyed up at the prospect of spending the day alone with Luke. Or rather as alone as any two adults could be hanging out on the beach with a rambunctious four-year-old.

I didn't know how I felt about tomorrow: excited, nervous, curious, terrified. If I were honest with myself, I would admit it was a mixture of all those things—some more, some less. But one emotion trumped all the others, so clear in my mind: relief. I was relieved that this wouldn't be the last time I saw either of the Sheridan guys.

Chapter Five

"Get over here, you four-footed, prima donna fur ball." Beside me, the kitchen faucet continued to pour its precious natural resource down the drain while Princess sat in the doorway having a staring contest with me. Winning, too. She probably wouldn't blink if a bottle rocket shot off in the kitchen.

"I said, come here, you little beast, and drink this water or you're going to have to slurp on your own spit until dinner."

Frustration must have buried my sense of self-preservation because I took two menacing steps toward the cat. The hiss drowned out even the sound of the pouring water. Swallowing, I retraced my steps back to safety on my own side of the room. When I was out of range of any waving claws, I tried my tough-gal role again.

"Well, if that's how you feel about it, then you'll have a thirsty afternoon." I made a big production of pushing down the handle to shut off the faucet. "See what meanness will get you?"

In the doorway, Princess still hadn't moved. She was watching me as if I was the most interesting thing she'd seen next to the flock of nasty seagulls that hung out on the beach.

Turning away, I filled the cat's bowl with fresh water and set it on her personalized place mat next to the counter. Though I might not have been her favorite person, I wasn't an animal, either. I know my aunt said her pet never drank from the bowl, but these were desperate times and maybe she would lower herself to the indignity of it.

How had I ever thought I could be a good parent? I couldn't even get a ten-pound cat to take a drink. I probably would have been just as much of a failure if I'd tried to convince a whining first grader to go to bed or tried to take the car keys from a belligerent teen. Maybe God had had a plan after all in denying me the thing I'd wanted most.

I popped the top off a single-serving can of gourmet cat food—this one ocean perch with salmon soufflé or some such—poured it into the porcelain bowl and set it next to the water, just as my aunt had demonstrated that morning.

Princess didn't bother to show any curiosity let alone come over and sniff her lunch. Instead, she turned tail and sauntered to parts unknown in the house.

"Fine," I called after her. "Don't eat anything. But you're going to get hungry if you keep this up until your mommy and daddy get home. Go take a nap, you ungrateful cat. Just go."

"But we just got here."

I whirled to see Sam with his face pressed against the slider screen. A baseball cap sat lopsided on his head, a ducky float ringed his waist and a frown pulled like gravity on his face. Next to him, Luke stood with a bag of sand toys hoisted over his shoulder.

Luke had his lips pressed together as if he was trying not to laugh. My face probably looked as though I'd made a fashion faux pas with a whole container of rouge.

"You want us to go?" Sam pressed, his eyebrows drawn together in confusion.

"Not you guys." I brushed my hand aside in frustration. "It's just—" I gestured toward the place where Princess had last sat. Of course, the spot beneath the door frame was empty now. "Oh, forget it."

"Ooooh-kay." Luke stretched out the word to its maximum length.

I shot a look toward the door again. "Oh. Sorry. Why don't you come in?"

Sam glanced back and forth a few times as if checking for danger before he risked opening the door. I understood just how he felt.

Luke followed him through the door. "Having some problems with the lady of the house?"

The look I shot him hit its mark before he even had time to hide his smirk. But I had to admit that the situation was laughable.

"Just a few," I answered finally.

Instead of poking fun at me as I expected he would, Luke strode past me into the great room. Dressed for the beach in a faded Michigan State T-shirt and a pair of long, royal-blue swimming trunks that matched his eyes, he started peering over and under things, lifting a pillow here and shifting a chair there. It dawned on me that he was hunting for the cat.

And without a top hat, a whip and a chair?

"Luke, wait—"

He wasn't listening, though. He was making this quick, clucking noise with his mouth.

"Here, kit, kit, kit."

"Do you have a death wish or what?" I blurted before I could stop myself.

Luke heard me that time, but he only lifted an eyebrow when he turned my way. If he thought Princess, reigning monarch of Bluffton Point Lighthouse and beyond, could be so easily tamed, then he had another thing coming.

"Daddy, I can help find the kitty," Sam announced in a youthful shriek that generally wouldn't attract small animals.

"That's okay, buddy." The volume of Luke's voice was only about a third of his son's. "Why don't you go out on the deck and scout the shoreline with the binoculars, so you can pick the best spot for us to put the beach umbrella?"

Sam shot through the door, barely taking enough time to open the screen.

"No going near the water without grown-ups, okay?" I called after him.

"Okay."

Luke nodded his agreement with my comment before returning to his study of places a cat might hide.

He found nothing under the end table, behind the curtains, even underneath the footrest of Uncle Jack's recliner. He had to open the chair to check that one.

Again, he started the clucking noise, following it with another round of *kit-kit-kit.*

To my utter shock, Princess reappeared in the kitchen doorway, looking at least a little intrigued. You mean clucking and *kit-kit-kit-ing* had worked better than my *little beasts* and *fur balls?*

"What do you need her to do?" he whispered to me though he was looking at the cat instead of me.

"Remember the drinks?"

His gaze drifted to the kitchen sink, and he nodded. With quiet steps in his sporty beach sandals, he moved in front of the sink and turned on the faucet. Backing up a little, he waited by the opposite counter.

Instead of staring at him the way she had me, the cat took a few tentative steps forward, and, seeming to sense there was no danger, padded into the kitchen and hopped on the counter. She batted the water a few times with her paw and then stuck her face under the stream for a long drink. When she was done, she hopped down from the counter, sauntered into the great room and plopped down next to the recliner to begin bathing herself.

I couldn't take my eyes off her. Had that just happened? And more importantly how had Luke made it happen? Not only was he an admirable, organized parent, Luke was also a regular Dr. Doolittle. I couldn't help being a tiny bit jealous of all that.

But I also was curious how Luke had accomplished

his trick with Princess. I was going to need this tidbit of information if the cat and I were going to survive the next twenty-one days together.

Twenty-one days and counting.

I turned my wide-eyed amazement on Luke, who had just shut off the faucet.

He smiled sheepishly. "I'm a cat person." He said it simply, as if that explained his sleight-of-hand performance to those of us who hadn't learned the art of feline love.

"What else do you need?" he asked.

I pointed to the bowl near his feet, the one still filled with food.

"I wouldn't worry about that. She'll eat when she's hungry. Cats won't starve themselves."

He walked back into the room where the cat lay, licking her paw and using it to clean her ear. She paused in her toilette to watch his careful approach, but she didn't bolt.

Soon, he'd crouched down beside her and was petting her head—all without the need for stitches. "Yeah, you'll be just fine, won't you girl? Just fine."

He paused in his crooning to look back at me. "I would be prepared for her not to eat much these first few days. Cats sometimes lose their appetites at first when their owners go away."

"I guess as long as she doesn't stop drinking, too."

Luke turned so he could pet his new friend and talk to me at the same time. "She won't. I would keep her water bowl full, though. Eleanor might think she never drinks from it, but Princess is probably just being sneaky.

If you had a good thing going like she does, would you go and mess it up by drinking out of your bowl?"

A chuckle bubbled up in my throat. "I never thought about it," I admitted, tongue pressed firmly in cheek.

"Well, cats, they think about such things."

"I'll remember that." I would have asked him how he had such insider knowledge into the minds of kitties, but the way Princess had closed her eyes and was pressing her nose into Luke's palm hinted that he knew about felines' preferences.

"Did you learn all those skills at MSU?" I pointed to his T-shirt. "It has a great veterinary science program."

"Me, a vet? Now that's funny. I studied business. For a while anyway." He glanced up at me again. "Why? Did you go to state?"

I shook my head. "University of Iowa for my bachelor's in speech and hearing sciences. Colorado State for a master's in communication."

"That's an awful lot of education."

"I guess." Because it seemed like overkill, I didn't mention that I'd also completed two internships in my field and then had to take a national exam to earn my certificate of clinical competence.

"You must like school a lot."

"I still work in one, don't I?"

The subject at its end, Luke returned his attention to the cat and started rubbing her ears. "You like that, don't you, Princess?"

As he spoke, he continued petting the fur on the cat's head in slow, mesmerizing circles that had her purring loudly. Who was I kidding? It nearly had *me* purring. I could just feel those massaging circles on my scalp. Would he brush his fingers through my hair, finding the strands soft from the new, leave-in conditioner I'd been using?

Plunk. I felt the rough landing in my thoughts. I really had reached rock bottom if I was jealous of a cat's head massage.

"Daddy and Miss Cassie, aren't you coming?"

Again, Sam was standing at the door, his face pressed against the screen, his bent hands forming a shade above his eyes.

Immediately, Princess shot up off the floor and scrambled out of the room. A tuft of short, white fur drifted to the hardwood floor where she'd been resting.

Luke plucked the hair off the floor as he stood and looked out the door at his son. "Did you find the perfect place for us to make camp?"

"Yeah. We'd better get it before someone takes it."

"Okay, let's hurry." Luke smiled over at me. Only the adults here understood that the exclusive beachfront real estate in this area included a private beach. The only public beach was farther down in the state park area surrounding the lighthouse. Sure, Lake Michigan was one of the Great Lakes and definitely public, but in some areas the only way to get access to the water was by skydiving in it.

"You two go ahead. I need to change." I'd been so focused on doing my kitty chores that I hadn't even gotten dressed for the beach. In my bedroom, I pulled on my simple teal-colored one-piece, regretting that I hadn't bothered to try it on before I left Toledo. The material hung a bit at my waist and hips, but it would have to do. The suit wouldn't matter because I intended to remain well covered all day. No more sunburns for me.

Zipping on my white cotton cover-up, I looked into the mirror to smooth down the hood. I topped off the getup with a floppy straw hat and movie-star sunglasses. I looked more like an ailing star, hiding from the paparazzi during recovery from a little nip and tuck.

I grabbed a paperback from the stack I'd brought for the trip and headed downstairs. Luke and Sam would probably want to swim. I hoped they wouldn't mind if I watched them play from beneath a beach umbrella. They would probably think I was a wallflower, but I couldn't help it. It wouldn't be wise for me to be frolicking in the water with that handsome father and his sweet little boy. It might make me wish for a life I could never have.

I brushed my fingers through my still-damp hair and shivered. Though the last golden shards of another sunset still lit the sky, it was already cold again. The air smelled clean instead of like other people's cooking, the way it always did in my third-floor apartment.

Because my teeth were chattering, I zipped my cover-up over my swimsuit. So much for my best-laid plans. I hadn't *planned* on going into the water, but then I couldn't have ordered a better day than the one I'd spent with Luke and Sam. My book and the umbrella had spent a lonely afternoon while I swam, chased, threw a football and, yes, even frolicked with the Sheridan guys.

Slipping my flip-flops on, I climbed the steps to the deck. I couldn't help smiling at the memory of Luke, who had looked all buff and tan from his outdoor work as he stood in the waist-high chilly water. Suddenly, Sam had leaped on his back causing Luke's knees to buckle, and they'd both disappeared into the water. I'd had a good laugh when they'd come up sputtering until Luke had grabbed Sam and had swum my way, giving me my own close-up view of the lake bottom.

"Is he up there?" Luke called now from beneath the deck.

"I'm checking inside."

Sam had gone up to the bathroom fifteen minutes before and hadn't returned, so I'd decided to investigate whether he was a victim of a Princess mauling.

"Sam, are you in here?" I called out as I entered the back door.

Silence. Now that was something I wasn't used to hearing when Sam was around. Anxiety balling in my stomach, I started hunting around for places a four-year-old boy might get into trouble. I didn't have to look long. On one of my aunt and uncle's cozy couches Sam was sacked out, a brightly colored beach towel still draped over his shoulders.

I headed back toward the deck just as Luke came through the door. He'd slipped on a sweatshirt and loose-fitting cotton pants over his swim trunks, and he carried a smaller set for his son.

"He's over there." I pointed to the couch.

Luke stared down at Sam, who had his face buried in the sofa cushion. "He does that sometimes. He just wears out and drops anywhere that looks comfortable. I should get him home."

"No, don't—" I wasn't sure what I'd been about to say, but I had a sinking suspicion it was something close to begging him to stay. What happened to my looking forward to time alone at my aunt's house?

Glancing back at the sleeping boy, I shrugged. "It's just…he looks so comfortable there. Maybe we should let him let him sleep for a while."

For several seconds, Luke studied his son as if considering, but finally he nodded. "I guess we could." He pointed outside. "I was just starting the fire."

"I'll go change."

He offered to feed Princess and give her a drink while he was waiting, and I gratefully took him up on the offer. I hurried up the stairs, nervous for the first time in hours. All day it had been just the three of us clowning and laughing together. Now it would be only two.

I slipped on a pair of jeans, a sweatshirt and sneakers and headed back outside. Cold as it was, my hands were sweating, so I wiped them on my pants.

Luke crouched next to the permanent fire pit that was encircled by a line of grapefruit-sized stones. He poked a stick into the flames, adjusting the logs that he'd stacked into a cone shape. He smiled at me, and I relaxed.

Settling back into one of the two camp chairs he'd arranged by the fire, he motioned for me to take the other. I lowered myself into it, letting the flames that licked over the firewood warm my toes, face and hands.

"How're my pyromaniacal skills?" he asked.

"Good job. What is it about guys and fire? What's the attraction?"

"God just wanted to make sure we'd figure out how to cook dinner." He poked his stick in the mound of smoldering logs again, and several pieces of glowing ash floated into the air.

"But then what guy cooks?"

"I cook."

I swallowed. Of course, he made meals for his family. He was a widower. Who else would do it? Leave it to me to say something that would make both of us uncomfortable.

"I'm sorry."

"Why? You haven't even tasted my cooking."

I let the breath I was holding out slowly, wondering if he could see the gratitude in my eyes. How could I have ever thought of him as a grouch. He was funny. More importantly, he was kind.

It wasn't even a far stretch to think that the two of us could possibly become friends. A person could always use more friends. And as his potential friend, I was curious to know more about him. About his wife. About his life since her death. But I couldn't come up with a good way to start a conversation.

He beat me to it. "Well, we both survived the whole wedding weekend, didn't we?"

I sighed loudly and laughed when I heard him do the same. "With no more than surface wounds."

His expression was serious, though, when he turned back to me in the firelight. "Weddings are always tough for me."

"Why? Because they remind you of your own wedding?"

Poking his stick into the fire again, he watched the spraying ashes for several seconds and then shook his head. "I don't believe in happily ever after."

"Oh." I tried to cover the surprise in my voice by clearing my throat. "You know my track record. I'd have to agree with you on that."

But how could we agree? My thoughts replayed bits of conversations from the last forty-eight hours. The poor, lonely widower raising his child alone. Something didn't fit, but maybe I was reading too much into it.

"I don't really know your track record. Only what my mom told me." He must have seen my eyes widen because he continued, "That your husband was a creep who left you for another woman."

"Don't sugarcoat it on my account," I said to get the laugh, though I appreciated that he'd stated it plainly. "She didn't tell you the rest?"

"It gets worse?"

"Or better, depending on how much you like sordid tales."

"I don't."

I glanced at him to see if he was joking. At first, his expression was serious, but finally the side of his mouth lifted. "But you can tell me anyway. If you want to."

Strange, I wanted to, and I hadn't wanted to tell this story to anyone since…well…ever. Most of the time, it felt as if the whole ugly ordeal had happened to someone else.

"I don't know where to begin."

"The beginning is good."

He was staring at me as if he really was interested in hearing the whole story. Had Alan ever wanted to know the whole story about anything? No, that was never necessary when the Cliffs Notes version would do.

"His name was Alan Whittinger." I almost added "from the Boston Whittingers" as if it mattered now—as if it ever should have mattered what pedigree Alan brought to our marriage and had taken with him when he left. "We've been divorced for two years now."

I half expected Luke's eyes to glaze over as I told him the pertinent details: Alan and I were married after dating two years, and we hadn't made it past our fourth anniversary. Luke, though, listened intently, as if it mattered. I liked that it mattered.

"Then he came home one day and announced that he was in love with the hostess at the restaurant where he spent so many business dinners. Not as much of a cliché as if she'd been his secretary, but close. He wanted to divorce me right away, so he could marry her. It was a good idea since she was seven months pregnant."

The last words burned my throat as I spoke them aloud. Even my aunt had been forced to pry the details of my divorce out of me, and here I'd laid them out like a grocery list for Luke. Admittedly, I hadn't shared the whole story, but not even Aunt Eleanor knew all of it.

I held my breath and waited, watching the flames casting shadows on his face. What I expected him to say I wasn't sure.

He shook his head. "Mom was wrong. *Creep* isn't a strong enough word for him."

"Ah, *creep* will do," I said with a laugh. That Luke had so quickly taken my side made me feel warm inside. If not for that prickly sense of doubt that suggested Alan might not have been the only one guilty for the failure of our marriage, I would have been content.

"You okay…with everything?"

Okay. That was such a vague term for a huge spectrum of possible feelings. Okay in that I would get by just fine, sure. Okay in that my trust in other human beings was as good as new—not so much.

"I guess." Then realizing my answer was as vague as his question, I added, "I'm a little scarred but still breathing in and out on a regular basis."

"From what I hear, that's the best way to breathe." He took a long breath of his own and stared out into the endless expanse of black water that was interrupted only by the occasional crash of white, foamy waves. "I know what scarred feels like."

At first, I wasn't sure I'd heard him correctly, especially since I'd guessed that his comment about breathing had been to lighten the conversation. But when he didn't follow with another punch line, I knew I'd heard right.

"In the mood to share?"

He shrugged. "What's to say? Nicole and I were college sweethearts. We married right after graduation—hers, not mine. I didn't finish. Anyway, we were still riding on a wave of optimism when we got married. We had a few good years and then had Sam, and he was great." A smile lifted his face at just the mention of his son. "But you can only ride a high for so long."

"I don't understand. What do you mean?"

Luke took a long time in answering, and when he did, he didn't look at me. "It would be easy for me to say Nicole was the only one who'd been quietly unhappy in our marriage. I couldn't blame her. I was a disappointment, I suppose. Anyway, I was as miserable as she was."

I could only stare at him. Everything he was telling me didn't seem possible. Why not? Because his wife had died? Why did I assume that her death gave them some retroactive immunity from marital problems? Clearly it hadn't. Luke shoved his hands back through his hair, leaving it standing up in places, but still he didn't look my way.

"Do you think you would have left her?" I asked.

"Not a chance!"

He said it with such vehemence that I couldn't help straightening in my seat. Something deep inside me told me he was telling the truth.

"Oh. Sorry."

Luke brushed my apology away with a wave of his hand and finally turned to me. "No, I'm sorry. I'm not even sure why I told you. With Nicole and me, it was probably just a rough patch, anyway. It would have passed. And if not," he paused long enough to shrug, "then—"

"You still would have stayed," I finished for him.

He appeared as surprised as I was that I'd said it. He nodded.

I wasn't even sure how I knew it, but I was convinced that if the sun had never shone again on their marriage, he still would have made the best of it. He was the kind of man who kept his commitments no matter what. Luke and I were little more than strangers—almost friends—and yet I felt as if I understood more about him than I'd ever known about the man I'd married.

"Now it's just Sam and me."

He was probably speaking more to himself than to me, and yet it felt as if he was offering me a reminder. Beyond being a loyal and forgiving person, he was a father. A wonderful father from what I'd seen. I wondered if he realized how attractive a single dad could be.

Luke didn't see himself as amazing; he'd made that much clear. He'd even mentioned his lack of a degree a few times and said that he'd disappointed his wife. How could a man like him ever have been a disappointment to himself or anyone else?

For a long time, I only watched him as he stared out into the night and, likely, into memories, both poignant and painful. My thoughts had drifted so far beyond this moment and this place that I didn't notice Luke turning toward me, but suddenly he was staring right at me.

I don't know if you would call it *awareness* or *attraction* that I was feeling, but I had an idea that the warmth spreading inside my chest had nothing to do with the flames popping nearby, and my hurrying pulse didn't suggest a heart attack. Did he feel it, or was I alone in my almost-thirty hot flash and heart arrhythmia?

I needed to look away from him, but I couldn't. Something in his eyes rooted me there, gazing back at him. Was it pain or loneliness, maybe the need for a friend? Those could have been things reflected from my own eyes, and because they probably were, I finally was able to break the connection.

"Just look at the two of us," I said with a chuckle. "Could Aunt Eleanor have chosen a more damaged pair to put in her wedding party if she tried?"

"Probably not."

"My picture's probably in one of those books on what *not* to do when you get married."

So much for my attempt to lighten the mood. I'd meant it to be funny, but he didn't laugh, and my own chuckle sounded forced. Making jokes about my dead marriage felt a little like hosting a comedy club at a cemetery—the monologue just as macabre.

Still, when I glanced up at Luke again, he was smiling, as if he, too, saw the humor and irony of our roles in my relatives' vows renewal. His smile made me forget the discomfort of a moment before, but it also made me forget my head. For me to feel this warm, this at peace with Luke wasn't a good idea. It made me imagine impossible things. It made me wonder what it would have been like if I'd met Luke before either of us had earned our scars.

Chapter Six

It had seemed like a good idea at the time. That was the only excuse I could come up with now for having suggested it last night. In the tall triangle of light that poured from the hallway into the spare bedroom, I peered over at the sleeping child who'd been in my care nearly twenty-four hours. Poor little boy. What was his father thinking?

When we'd finally extinguished the fire and returned to the house, Sam had been sleeping so soundly that I'd told Luke it was a shame to wake him. I'd said it would be fun to have Sam sleep over so we could play all day Monday together on the beach. Playing house and pretending to be Sam's mom hadn't sounded half-bad, either, but I'd kept that to myself. I'd felt a twinge of guilt for my plan then, but not anymore.

In Luke's defence, he'd called around five-thirty that night and said something had come up at work and he'd be a little late. If this was a little late, what would be a lot, a week from next Thursday?

"Miss Cassie," Sam whispered from across the room.

"You were supposed to be sleeping, you little sneaker."

"I miss my sunshine." Sam lifted his head and, planting his elbow on the pillow, propped his arm under it. "I'm thirsty, too. I need a drink of water."

"A drink, huh? Didn't you already have one a while ago?"

"Yes, but I need another one." He sat up in the massive four-poster bed that made him look even smaller than usual. He was wearing one of my T-shirts as a nightshirt. That had been the best I could do while I threw the rest of his clothes in the wash. Even Luke's plan-ahead bag hadn't been stocked with enough clothes for a two-night getaway.

"I bet Princess needs a drink, too," he added, looking at me hopefully.

Now this boy knew how to press his point. He also knew my weakness. All day that mangy feline had continued to snub my efforts, but she'd let a four-year-old talk her into a few sips of water. I'd been careful to keep the bowls filled, but Princess wouldn't give me the satisfaction of eating a bite when I could see her. The cat was spoiled and sneaky, angry and aloof—a royal pain as far as I was concerned.

Twenty days and counting.

"Well, if it's only for Princess's sake, then I guess it's okay."

The boy nearly leaped out of the bed. Where did he get his energy? After all those hours in the sun—the swimming, the sand castle building and that fiasco playing beach volleyball—he should have been ready to drop. I knew I was.

I expected Sam to stall after he padded to the kitchen, but he drank the whole cup of water I gave him and turned the faucet back on for Princess. This time no amount of four-year-old persuasion could bring the cat out of hiding, but Sam didn't take it as personally as I had.

"I guess she isn't thirsty," he said with a shrug.

"Guess not. Come on. Let's get you back to bed." Taking his hand, I led him back to the stairs. "Do you need to go to the bathroom before you go back to bed?"

"Nope."

Tucking Sam in a second time, I kissed him on the forehead. He smelled of soap and the baby shampoo I'd bought just for tonight's bath.

"Good night again, little man."

"Good night."

I stepped out the door and started to pull it shut behind me. Not completely closed. I already knew better than that from my first attempt at putting Sam to sleep. Either afraid of the dark or just nervous about going to sleep in a strange place, he'd asked me to leave on the hall light. We'd already said his prayers together the first time I'd put him to bed, so God would probably forgive us if we didn't do double duty.

"Miss Cassie."

"Yes, Sam." No more drinks. This time I was going to have to put my foot down or he would be up and down all night.

"When is my daddy coming?"

"Soon, sweetheart. Sleep well."

It was all I could do to keep from stomping down the

hall. As if it wasn't bad enough that Luke had left his son in my care longer than any self-respecting parent ever would have, now he'd put me in a position of having to possibly lie to Sam.

I had no idea when Luke would return to collect his son or even if— No, that wasn't fair, but I wasn't feeling all that generous right now.

And I wasn't feeling any more inclined to it forty-five minutes later when I finally heard an engine and the thud of a vehicle door outside. I almost went to the front door to open it before Luke rang the bell and awakened his son, but then I realized he wouldn't go to the door like a stranger when he'd already been welcomed into this house like a friend. Whether he could still be called one of those depended on his answers to some questions in the next few minutes.

"Knock. Knock," he called from outside the screened slider. "May I come in?"

At least he had the good sense not to walk right in. That would have sent me right over the edge. Not trusting myself to speak, I remained seated on the sofa and motioned for him to come inside. Luke stood just inside the door, looking about as beat as I felt. His hair was a straggly mess from his worrying it too much with his hands, and his five o'clock shadow had taken on ten o'clock haggardness.

He must have read the anger in my eyes or noticed my jaw that I couldn't seem to loosen because he rushed to explain. "Hey, I'm so sorry about this. I never intended to leave you in the lurch. I didn't have any idea it would take this long. Minor job crisis. You know how those go."

As a matter of fact, I did. I'd had those days when the school roof leaked, leaving my shelves of reference books in jeopardy, or when a student had come to school with signs of abuse and I'd been obligated to call Child Protective Services. I wasn't about to share those stories now, though. The last thing Luke Sheridan needed was someone to commiserate with him. More than anything he needed to get the lecture that was coming to him.

Before I could begin it, Luke prattled on with his apology, as if anything he said was going to make what he'd done okay.

"It's just that the township is taking its sweet time in approving some of the permits. Here I've got several subcontractors lined up, and we have no permits for them to start the job."

He stopped, probably waiting for me to tell him how badly I felt for him. Wrong answer. One of the Sheridan guys deserved my pity, but I hated to tell Luke he wasn't the one.

As nonchalantly as possible, I stood up from the couch and started fluffing its pillows. Over my shoulder, I asked, "Don't you want to know how your son is?"

"What?" He shook his head, my question clearly surprising him. Crossing to the kitchen, he leaned his elbows heavily on the counter. "Of course I do. How is Sam?"

I followed him into the kitchen, but instead of joining him at the counter, I stepped to the sink and loaded Sam's water glass into the dishwasher.

"He's fine. He had some grilled chicken for dinner, he's had a bath, and he's sleeping upstairs."

"Thanks. I really appreciate it."

"Somebody had to do it," I said with a shrug.

Luke's posture stiffened, his jaw tightening. He was becoming angry? A few people here had the right to be mad, but he wasn't one of them.

"Look, I said thanks. I'm sorry that things turned out the way they did. I didn't mean—"

"You didn't mean to leave your son waiting here until after ten o'clock?"

He shook his head, his frustration palpable. "It couldn't be avoided. I told you that."

"Don't worry about it. I guess it couldn't be helped."

"I said I'm sorry."

I raised my hand to stop him. "No, it's fine. Really."

"Don't...do that." His voice sounded so strange, and he appeared to be gritting his teeth.

"What are you talking about?"

"Quit playing the martyr. If you're mad, be mad. If you have something to say, then say it."

At first I just stared at him, but then I straightened my shoulders. "I'm mad."

"You have every right to be. When I called, I didn't know I would be so late."

"Another call wouldn't have been too much to ask."

Luke nodded. "Point taken. I just got caught up in the problems, and I wanted to prove I could handle them." He paused, flexing his jaw. "But none of that matters. I should have been here."

Pushing back from the counter, he brushed his hands together as if he considered the matter settled. Maybe I should have left it at that. He'd admitted he was wrong, and that should have been enough for me. But I never could let sleeping dogs lie when I could make my point better by nudging the little pooches with my foot.

"I would think your job is pretty demanding."

He smiled as if he appreciated the change in subject. "You've got that right."

"You probably work a lot of hours." Though I'd kept my comment carefully vague, Luke's smile disappeared, and he raised an eyebrow.

"Enough," he answered, equally vague.

I considered stopping there; really I did. But I'd seen so much questionable parenting while working with at-risk children, parents who just couldn't be bothered to attend to their children's basic needs. I might have a chance to make a difference in this one child's life, and I just had to do it.

"How many days a week would you say you work late?"

His hands gripped the edge of the counter this time, and he trapped me in his narrowed gaze. "Just what are you getting at, Cassie?"

I shrugged as if the subject were something far more casual than a little boy's emotional stability. "Sam said usually when you're working late, he stays at his grandparents' house."

"He loves it at Grammy and Papa's."

"I'm sure he does. It's just that—"

"What, do you have trouble with family members providing day care? You're probably one of those proponents of institutionalized day care centers. You're convinced my child will suffer socially if he's not corralled with twenty other four-year-olds and required to nap each day at one-fifteen."

I started shaking my head before he was finished. "No, that's not it." I did have some definite ideas about child care and quality preschool instruction, but it might not be good to impart all of my knowledge at once.

"Then what is it?" He braced his arms so stiffly, it was as if he expected a blow rather than my words.

"I just wonder, if you're working late all the time, then maybe you're putting your career first while leaving your parents to raise Sam."

Why did it feel as if suddenly all the nighttime sounds from outside had disappeared at once? Luke turned so his back was to me, but his jaw was tight, and I was almost certain I saw a vein ticking at his temple.

The silence unnerving me, I tried again. "It's just that I see this happen in my job. Parents work hard so that their children will have *more,* and what they really need is more time with their parents."

"That's what you think, huh?" He said it with a chuckle, but when he turned back to me, his expression was about as far from smiling as it could come without surgical assistance.

That combined with the anger that radiated from him in waves had me taking a step back from his penetrating gaze. He didn't step forward, didn't take an intimidating stance of any sort, but I still was tempted to back out of the room because I probably wouldn't like whatever he was about to say.

"Do you have any idea how many people feel obligated to give me suggestions about raising Sam? Poor, lonely widower. He couldn't possibly have a clue how to raise his own son."

Recognizing I'd stepped over the line, I lifted my hands wide. "Look, I was just trying to…"

"Help." We both said it at the same time, but it sounded feeble coming from my mouth.

"For three years now, I've had people coming out of the woodwork like termites going to a two-by-four feast, every one of them wanting to *help.* My parents, my in-laws, people at church, strangers at the grocery store. Everybody's got a tip for the poor widower."

He paced away from me, his arms crossed, only to whip around and face me again. "Sam is *my* son. It's *my* job to decide how to raise him."

"Of course he's your son."

"And yet everyone on the Michigan coast of the Big Lake thinks he knows more about what *my son* needs that I do."

I had no doubt that this "everyone" he spoke of was referring to me, but at least he hadn't singled me out.

"I'm sorry. I shouldn't have…" I let my words trail off because we both knew what I shouldn't have said.

He nodded as if to acknowledge my apology. "But it gets even worse," he continued. "Now I not only have parents offering me their gems of experience, I'm supposed to be grateful when I get tips from people who don't even have kids."

Again he didn't name me. He didn't have to. He was right. Whether or not he'd messed up tonight—and I still was convinced he had—I had no business making assumptions about his whole life with his son. Just because I'd seen some examples of poor parenting at my school didn't mean I knew anything about Luke and Sam.

"Really, Luke, forgive me. I had no right."

Luke just raised his hand to stop me and stepped past me into the great room. "I'm the one who gets him up every morning and puts him to bed every night," he said without looking back. "I know that Sam would rather take a long walk off a short pier than eat his green beans and that he prefers to sleep with a monkey named Sunshine."

"Sunshine?"

He turned to face me, looking more tired now than angry. "It's just this stuffed monkey with matted gray fur. A real eyesore."

"I thought he was talking about missing the sun outside, not a toy named Sunshine." I shook my head, finally laughing at myself when I should have been chortling all along instead of taking myself so seriously.

"You see what I mean? I'm Sam's dad. I know him. I know the important things, like that he's afraid of the dark and daddy longlegs and that he has accidents if he doesn't go to the bathroom right before—"

"Oh, my gracious," I interrupted him, already rushing for the stairs.

"Let me guess. He talked you into letting him get a drink."

I'd climbed the first few steps, but I turned back to him, frowning. "No. Two."

"Well, better join Noah and the animals in the ark because another great flood is coming."

* * *

As it turned out, there was no sign of a second Noah or any animals traveling two by two. Sam wasn't even in his bed when I reached his room at a flat-out run. He'd made it back to the bed, given fair warning by my herd-of-buffalo approach, but the boy just couldn't manage to scramble under the covers before I threw the door wide.

I flipped on the light, crossed my arms and drew my eyebrows together, waiting.

"Did Daddy come?" His gaze darted to the side as he said it.

"You know he did, Sam." I didn't add *you little stinker* to my comment, but I was too busy trying to replay my conversation with Luke. What had we said that might permanently damage a child? Some of it had stung even my pride, and I was technically an adult.

"I'm here, buddy." Luke said from behind me. He didn't bother to call Sam on his stretch of the truth, and he didn't apologize for anything his son might have overheard, either. "It's late, though. You need to go to the bathroom, and then we need to get home."

Funny, I don't know why, but I expected Sam to balk, to beg to stay another night and spend another day playing with me. So it surprised as much as stung me when he stood up on the bed and held out his arms for his father to take him. In three long strides, Luke was with him, but instead of lifting him immediately, Luke tugged at the sleeve of the oversize T-shirt, covered in tie-dyed frogs.

He glanced back at me. "Where are his clothes?"

"I washed them. You can take that home and return it later."

"That's all right. Where are his things now?"

"In the dryer. I'll get them." I hurried from the room as if he was chasing me. I didn't have to pretend I didn't understand why he needed Sam's clothes right away and didn't want to take mine: he didn't want any reason to come back here.

Once a sleepy Sam had taken a restroom break and was back in his own clean things, Luke gathered his son in his arms and strode down the hallway.

I followed after him. "It was great having you here, Sam."

"Thank you," the boy said, already snuggling sleepily into the comfort of his father's arms. They were at the bottom of the steps when Sam's head popped up again. "Tell Princess goodbye for me, okay?"

"I will."

Luke glanced back at me, his silence speaking louder than his words ever could. Here I'd been trying to tell him how to care for his child, and we both knew I still hadn't mastered Pet Care 101.

I kind of hoped he would smile, would see the humor in the situation, even if I was having a hard time finding it myself. He didn't. Instead, he continued across the room to the slider, only turning back to me when his hand was on the door. "Thanks for spending the day with Sam."

I cleared my throat. "It was my pleasure."

He tapped the side of his head against Sam's mop of hair. "Say bye to Miss Cassie."

"Bye, Miss Cassie."

Sam lifted his hand for a sleepy wave and then let it fall back on his father's arm. His smile was the last thing I saw as Luke carried him out the door. The sound of the slider clicking closed had a disconcerting finality to it.

After they disappeared around the side of the house, I stared out at the deck, its stained cedar planks golden in the artificial light. The wooden structure appeared larger now that it was empty except for a few groupings of tan and navy patio furniture. The laughter and smiles that had populated the deck and the rest of this house for the last several days were starkly absent.

But it was more than the empty house that made me feel so vacant inside. I missed the noise, the activity and the laughter that came with Luke Sheridan and his rambunctious son. After tonight, I would probably see neither of them again, and it was mostly my fault.

"How's my precious princess doing?"

I grinned into the portable phone Wednesday afternoon, only a little disappointed that it was an international call I'd answered rather than a local one. I shouldn't have expected any different. If Luke were going to call, he would have done it by now, instead of leaving me for the last two days to relax my body, bake my skin and generally go out of my mind with trying to avoid sessions of introspection. This was supposed to be a time for respite, not an episode of "Cassie Blake—This is Your Life."

Though my grin had long since faded, I remained determined to stay cheerful. "How's your princess doing? That depends. Are you talking about me or the cat?"

"Both, of course." Aunt Eleanor's laughter warmed

me, even through four thousand miles as the jumbo jet flies.

"But for now tell me about my kitty. Jack made me wait forever before I could check in with you."

If that wasn't the definition of irony, I didn't know what was. This was the third time she'd phoned me since they'd left for Paris. If she called any more often, she would have to mortgage her mansion to pay the cell phone bill.

"She's fine. Really."

Well, she wasn't dead. I knew that anyway. In fact, Princess was sitting in the doorway to my guest suite that minute, watching me chatting on the phone and putting away the rest of my clean laundry in the bureau drawers.

For a cat that despised me, she sure spent a lot of time watching me. That morning my heart had skipped a few important beats when I'd awakened to find her sitting on the end of the bed, just watching. But then didn't most of the big cats study their prey before they attacked?

Eighteen days and counting.

"Cassandra Eleanor, are you listening? I'm paying a pretty penny for all this dead air."

I cleared my throat. "Oh. Sorry. Now what were you saying?"

"I asked if she was eating okay."

"She's eating." She hadn't exactly done it in my presence, but there did appear to be a good-sized dent in each little mound of food when I threw out the left-overs. That was proof as far as I was concerned, unless an industrious ant colony had figured out a way to score three squares a day.

"Is she getting enough water?"

"Sure." At least I hoped so.

"Have the two of you finally become friends?"

How was I supposed to answer that one without lying? I might have gotten out of the habit of attending church, but that didn't mean I didn't believe in the Ninth Commandment.

"We sure are getting to know each other better," I said finally. *Whew, that was a close one.*

"Wait," Eleanor said. "You said 'depends.' If Princess is fine, then what's the matter with you?"

Now that would be hard to determine without a team of counselors and a truckload of chocolate truffles thrown in for good measure. But I only said, "I'm fine, too."

"Have you gotten any sun?"

"Yes, and I have enough freckles to prove it."

"Not too much, right? You're wearing your sunscreen?"

"Always."

"And a hat."

"Sometimes."

I smiled again. My aunt and I had shared many conversations like this one, and it was great to see that even an ocean couldn't stop her from mothering me.

"Have you seen any more of Sam this week?"

My breath hitched. She was good, my aunt. She'd started a fishing expedition, using Sam as the lure and not even mentioning Luke. Well, I could be a slippery fish when I wasn't in the mood to be caught.

"Sam had a sleepover here. We had a great time."

"Oh really," she said in a tone that convinced me I was dangling from a hook even as we spoke.

"What are you saying?"

"I'm just surprised Luke let Sam stay over. He doesn't usually let anyone get close to his son. He doesn't appreciate everyone's well-meaning advice, either. Even Yvonne has learned to keep her opinions on parenting to herself unless Luke asks for them."

Well, that little tidbit had arrived a few days too late to help me at all. "Oh," I said before I could stop myself.

"What does 'oh' mean? Did Luke tell you to mind your own business, too?"

"Of course not." No, not in so many words.

"Look, Aunt Eleanor, Luke is a nice enough man, and if I were in the market…"

I let my words fall away. If I were in the market, what? Would I have been completely intrigued by him? Would I have been equally disappointed he hadn't called? As I was now, for example.

"But you're not in the market."

"No, I'm not."

She took that blow to her matchmaking plans with much more aplomb than I expected. If such a thing were possible, I would think my aunt had overdosed on aplomb today.

We said our goodbyes, and I hung up the phone, casting the house into its strange summer silence again. It was too late in the day to hear the warblers singing and too early for the cicadas to begin their noisy night-time dance.

Why I had ever looked forward to three weeks alone

in the sun and sand, I couldn't say. The Lake Michigan water was too cold in June to soothe my soul. The sand between my toes only chafed my skin, and running across the beach in the heat of the day felt like a barbecue for toes. Even the sunsets—okay, the sunsets were beautiful enough to convert an atheist and give him the call to the ministry the same day, but that was beside the point.

So what was the point, that I hated being alone? No, that couldn't be it. I was a veteran of *aloneness*. To the outsider, I probably made it seem downright festive. I just missed activity, I guessed. The sheer busyness of my life had served as wonderful insulation from thoughts and feelings, and here without it, I felt exposed.

Now don't get me wrong. I'd fought off this need to look inward the best I could. I'd watched Elvis in *Blue Hawaii* and Sidney Poitier in *To Sir, with Love*—two of my absolute favorites.

I'd also caught up all the laundry, dusted, vacuumed and cleaned all the bathrooms, even the ones I'd had to traipse around the place to locate. My aunt's wood blinds, the ones that filtered some of the morning sun on the east-facing windows, had probably never been as clean as they were after my attack with first the feather duster and then the lemon oil.

No wonder Princess just followed me from room to room, watching me perform like a domestic goddess and Olympic speed skater all rolled into one, but a gal had to do what a gal had to do.

I was running, all right. I had to if I planned to stay ahead of this sense that God was using this silence, this water, this place to make me take an internal inventory. Was this how Jonah felt when he was avoiding God's command to work in Nineveh? Would I end up in a whale's belly, too, if I didn't stop running?

Okay, I'd lost it after all. Just the image of me sitting in a puddle of whale digestive juices waiting to be spit back out made me grin. There wasn't a whale to be found in Lake Michigan, and a forty-pound salmon might try the whole swallowing thing, but he wouldn't get the job done.

All kidding aside, there was only so much more of this I could take. If I had to stay here alone one more day, I probably would have to give in and listen to what God had to say.

Chapter Seven

By late Friday night, I lay spent on one of the padded deck chairs, my bare feet heavy on the wood decking and a floppy hat pulled low on my face to block out any light, natural or otherwise.

I almost wished I could have found one of those imaginary Lake Michigan whales. I already felt as if I'd been swallowed and spit back up, and I hadn't even gotten a water ride out of it. Self-examination was exhausting. A warning should have been posted on the whole activity: Not recommended for the faint of heart.

There was nothing like having a clear villain and a clear victim in a drama and discovering that, oops, the victim wasn't guilt-free. But this wasn't a purse snatching or a random act of violence. It had taken two of us to make our marriage and two to break it.

Not that I was ready yet to divide the responsibility fifty-fifty with my ex-husband or anything. I wasn't the one who'd played musical beds and made procreation an extramarital party game. But I had chosen my husband for all the wrong reasons: why would I want boring qualities like honesty, reliability or a strong faith when I could have a man who was as ambitious as I was and a whole lot more charismatic? She who sows weeds, reaps—surprise, surprise—weeds.

I'd had weeds, all right, big, gnarly weeds with thorns and the smell of decay to boot. That I'd had a part in making them grow shamed me.

"Dear God," I said aloud, beginning another of my stilted prayers that I'd been attempting for the last forty-eight hours. "You know me…well, you used to anyway. I'm sorry. Please forgive me. We haven't talked in a while, but—I don't know what to say to…"

I let my words trail off. I had no idea what to say to the God of the Universe, my God with whom I'd once shared such a comforting intimacy. Until now, I hadn't realized how much I'd missed that closeness and what had always felt like two-way conversations with Him.

"I want that again, Father," I whispered, pushing back my hat and sitting up in the seat. Already, dozens of stars sparkled in the sky that was deepening to a blue-violet. Out of my peripheral vision, I recognized the outline of the lighthouse, casting its own triangular spray of light in various directions.

When I'd first arrived, I'd found the lighthouse majestic, but now I had to reserve that word for the night sky, enormous and unencumbered by jutting man-made structures. With spots of light that spattered across that ever-darkening backdrop, God had provided safe passage for those who traveled by water long before the first brick of Bluffton Point Lighthouse had been mortared.

The sky stretched on until it and the water touched at the horizon, just as God's love seemed to be touching me. He was here with me; I could feel it. I should have been chilly now that the sun was gone, but I was surrounded in warmth. God had been with me all along, I realized now. He'd just been waiting for me to notice.

I was sitting in the dark, more at peace with myself than I'd been in months when the phone rang to fracture the silence. As tired as I'd been, I hadn't even remembered to bring the portable phone outside with me, so I had to run inside to answer it.

"She must be getting desperate now," I told a disinterested Princess as I passed her on my way to the kitchen extension. What time was it in Paris? I counted off the six-hour time difference. Aunt Eleanor was calling at three o'clock in the morning?

I flipped on the handset and spoke before my aunt had the chance. "Shouldn't you be in bed?"

"I guess, but I usually try to stay up at least a few hours after I tuck Sam in."

The next snide remark I'd intended to give to my pet-loving aunt caught in my throat. "Luke?"

"Expecting someone else?" His voice had taken on a tone I didn't recognize.

If didn't know better, I would have thought I'd heard a note of disapproval in his voice, as if he wasn't happy to think I'd had been expecting someone else's call. Though my ears were probably just ringing from an overdose of self-examination, I couldn't help being pleased by the thought.

"I figured it was Aunt Eleanor calling again, checking in on her beloved cat."

"Again?"

"Since she left, she's called more frequently than a telemarketer offering a great deal on long distance."

"That often, huh?"

"That often."

Maybe I should have asked Luke why he'd phoned now when four nights ago he couldn't get away from me fast enough, but that would only make him hang up now. That was the last thing I wanted him to do. I didn't want to analyze it, to pick apart why I wanted to spend more time with a man who'd already made it clear he wasn't interested in me. I just wanted to keep talking.

Only we weren't talking.

The silence stretched too long, and for the life of me I couldn't come up with anything clever to say. Should I ask how Sam was doing? No, Luke might think I was judging his parenting skills again.

How about mentioning his mother or my aunt? I shook my head. That would only make him remember a certain matchmaking scheme, and I didn't plan to go *there.* I might have been desperate for human interaction, but I wasn't a suicide conversationalist.

"How is the cat doing, anyway?" he said finally.

I shrugged as I pinned the phone between my ear and shoulder. Though that wasn't the subject I would have chosen, it was something. "We're both alive."

"Alive is good."

Sixteen days and counting.

Again, the silence hung heavily around me. What

was he waiting for, another apology from me? I was forming the best one I could come up with after the day I'd spent when he spoke again.

"Sam misses you."

Now that I hadn't expected. "Oh." I cleared my throat. Was this a test? Had Luke brought up Sam's name just to see if I would head off on another diatribe about how he should raise his son? "I…um…miss him, too."

"He's been begging to see you every night this week."

"That's sweet."

"He's also been throwing terrible tantrums."

"Oh," I said again. Forget suicide conversationalist, when had I lost the ability to speak in full sentences? I was a speech path, of all things. How was I supposed to help students with their fluency disorders when I couldn't string more than two syllables together myself? Would my parents think they'd wasted all that college tuition money if they could see me now?

"I promised him if he could behave for one night, I would call you and we would try to see you this weekend."

I didn't even bother answering this time because whatever I said would probably sound curiously like "oh."

"I know what you're thinking. I'm a lousy parent, bribing my kid just so I can get him to go to bed."

"You don't know what I'm thinking." If he did know, he'd realize I still hadn't gotten past the part where he'd mentioned seeing me again. And if he could see me right now, he'd see how ridiculous I looked patting my hair into place when we were only talking on the phone.

"But bribing is lousy parenting," he continued. "You know that's true."

"The truth is, you know how little I know about parenting." I took a deep breath and added, "You made that clear the other night."

"Maybe you haven't been a parent, but you've had a lot of experience with kids, and you've helped plenty of them."

"Thanks for saying that."

"Why? It's just the truth."

I cleared my throat, embarrassed as much as flattered by his praise. He was right; everything he'd said about me was true, and yet his words validated my work in a way that the ambitious professional goals that Alan and I shared never had.

"Cassie, I'm really sorry about the other night."

Just like everything else about this conversation, I hadn't expected an apology from him. "No, I'm the one who should be sorry."

"Fine. It's a tie."

I smiled into the receiver. "Yes. Let's make a truce."

"That calls for a truce dinner. We can do it tomorrow. You provide the awesome lake house, and I'll bring the food and man the grill."

"Well, that's one way of garnering an invitation," I said with a laugh.

"My son had to get his lousy manners somewhere."

"You go, Dad."

But I wasn't offended, and he knew it. Over the next

few minutes we finalized plans for dinner. I even suggested that we make a day of it, just the three of us, so we could help Sam work on his swimming. Luke didn't sound all that enthusiastic when he agreed, but it was probably just my ringing ears again.

After ending the call, I hurried through what was already becoming my nighttime routine of locking up the house, scooping Princess's litter and putting out fresh water and food. I didn't waste time or water by running the faucet, and the cat didn't bother to sniff the food she would reject, anyway, until after I went to bed. At least female and feline could agree to disagree.

I crawled into bed, pulled up the lightweight comforter and waited for sleep to hit me like a bag of rocks. After a draining day like this one had been, I deserved some serious shut-eye. Twenty minutes later, though, I was still lying there, having counted all one hundred sixty-seven swirls in the plaster ceiling design and having given up on counting sheep because they were stampeding.

Why was I so keyed up, anyway? Tomorrow would only be another sunny afternoon with Luke Sheridan and his son. At least the forecasters predicted a sunny afternoon, which meant I had better find the galoshes and umbrellas just in case. But my uneasiness had little to do with the weather forecast, the predicted water temperature or even small-craft warnings. It had to do with the prospect of spending time with two special guys I'd been missing all week.

This was just silly, I decided as I flipped over, fluffed my pillow for the umpteenth time and buried my face in the center of it. Maybe I should take this anxiousness or excitement or whatever it was as a warning that tomorrow wasn't such a good idea.

Was I becoming more involved with the Sheridan family than was wise? If I had any sense at all I would call Luke back, wish him well and say a quick goodbye. That would probably be best. Fast goodbyes just weren't polite, though, and no one could accuse me of being impolite. Mom had taught me well. So the decision was made: I would see the Sheridan guys as planned. No one would accuse me of having any sense, either.

"Watch this, Miss Cassie."

At the bottom of the deck steps, I turned to look back at the beach. Sam was still crouched next to the sand castle village he and I had spent the last hour building. He stood and, with the handle of his pail in one hand and a red shovel in the other, spun in low-flying helicopter fashion, whacking all of our best towers as he went.

"Smack! Crash! Boom!"

I waited until his sound effects were finished before commenting on his work. "Boy, you tore all that down faster than we could build it."

"I'm really strong."

"You sure are. Sand castle villagers beware."

When he started spinning again, sending sand flying in all directions, I hurried for cover, continuing up the steps. On the deck, Luke stood next to a stainless steel gas grill wider than my car and with enough side burners and other gadgets that it should have marinated, cooked and served the meat all by itself. That little toy was probably my uncle's pride and joy.

Luke appeared right at home as master of the barbecue, wearing a gaudy Hawaiian shirt open over his T-shirt and a red half apron tied loosely over his swim trunks. He topped the ensemble off with a MSU baseball cap, worn backward, and dark sunglasses. The whole getup should have been ridiculous, but somehow he made the look work for him. Who was I kidding? Luke Sheridan could show up wearing a pink tutu and a tiara and still come off looking unusually handsome and utterly masculine.

"What are you smiling at?"

I pressed my lips together, trying to stop, but that just made me want to laugh. How was I supposed to answer his question? Even if I avoided the whole tutu subject, I couldn't mention how pleased I was that I'd ignored my misgivings and hadn't canceled our date.

Date? This certainly didn't qualify as one unless the definition had changed since the last time I was single to include a miniature chaperone, but I couldn't help wishing a little. Who knew the next time I'd meet someone who could make a blue Hawaiian shirt with huge white daylilies splattered all over it work the way Luke did.

"Okay. Keep your secret. See if I care."

I answered him with an exaggerated shrug. "Too much sun, probably." That was true, too, and Aunt Eleanor would have been disappointed to see I wasn't even wearing a hat. My hair was flying around like a mop of straw, and it would probably take a rake to detangle it by bedtime.

"Did you have fun building sand castles?"

"Sure, but I think I know how architects feel after a natural disaster."

Luke chuckled. "I just had a nice visit with Princess. I gave her lunch by the way. And she took a nice long drink from the faucet."

My frown must have spoken volumes because he laughed again. "She's still not performing her tricks for you?"

"Except the hissing one, no."

He shrugged. "She looks healthy enough, so she's not starving or anything. As long as she's using her litter box, then she's doing just fine."

"That's what I figured."

"Don't worry. You'll grow on her, sooner or later."

"Fifteen days and counting." I didn't realize I'd said my daily affirmation aloud until he looked back at me and tilted his head to the side.

"What's that?"

"It's the number of days until I'm outta here."

"I see" was all he said, and I didn't know whether to be relieved or disappointed. He didn't appear to be upset that I wouldn't be here long, but the fact that I wished it bothered him wasn't a good sign.

"You see him?" Luke pointed with the oversize, manly man metal spatula at the junior tornado on the beach. "That's my boy. I bet he'll be a demolition crew foreman when he grows up."

Sam was still spinning, but there was nothing left of our

village as far I as I could tell. "Only if he gets to be the one operating the wrecking ball or detonating the explosives."

"You know him well."

I turned back to him, needing to know if he was being serious or just reminding me of our discussion the other night and how *little* I knew his son. But he was smiling. When he didn't look away immediately, my cheeks warmed, but I couldn't help smiling back at him.

"Just a guess," I answered.

Glancing away, Luke pushed back the lid of the grill and turned the hot dogs he'd brought for Sam. Why anyone would choose meat by-products and fillers instead of a big slab of steak I would never understand. I'd just come to the conclusion that it had to be a kid thing when Luke spoke again over his shoulder.

"I thought a lot about the things you said the other night."

"Look, Luke, I really overstepped my boundaries that night, and—"

"And you were right about a lot of things," he said, interrupting me and finishing my sentence with his own take on the subject. "My spending too much time at work and away from Sam, for instance."

He patiently turned several more hot dogs. Just how many could one little boy eat? And just how long could the boy's dad pause before finishing what he'd started to say.

Finally, he lowered the spatula and turned back to me. "I'd told myself it was okay because Sam wasn't with strangers. He had family members around him whenever he wasn't with me."

"It is good that he has the chance to spend time with Marcus and Yvonne," I threw in, not certain why I defended him now when the other night I'd been so critical of him.

With nervous hands, I captured my mop in a temporary ponytail at my nape. "Do you know how blessed he is to have grandparents living nearby? Or to have living grandparents at all?"

"He's lucky to have them, especially now that Nicole is gone, but that doesn't take away my responsibility as his dad. He needs me most of all, and I need to make him my priority."

"Yes, but—"

"Yes but nothing. I dropped the ball here, and I wanted to thank you for reminding me to pick it up."

He paused long enough to open the grill again and turn the slabs of red meat. "How do you like your steak? Still mooing? Charred to ashes?"

"How about somewhere in between those two, but more toward the ashes side than the mooing one, okay?"

I stepped closer and examined his progress as he sliced into the T-bones with a knife. They were still too pink for my taste. Removing the hot dogs, he placed them on a platter he'd covered in foil, and then he sealed them with a second piece of foil before setting the platter on the grill's counter area. He removed some other food and set it aside, keeping it warm on another foil-covered platter.

I waited until he'd closed the lid and laid aside his

grilling tools before I spoke again. "You're welcome, I guess. About the reminder." It pleased me more than I cared to admit that he'd valued my advice.

Stepping to the deck's railing and resting his forearms on the expanse of wood, Luke studied his son playing on the sand below us. I settled beside him, letting the wind off the water push my hair back from my face. Neither of us seemed to need conversation for a few minutes as we let the serenity of the place envelop us.

At least that was what I was doing. I wondered what Luke thought when he saw this sun, this sand and this vast pool of water that God had formed with His own hands. A week ago, I remembered Luke mentioning they had to get up for church, so maybe he'd already noticed God's handprints on this place before I'd opened my eyes to see them.

I almost expected him to mention those awesome handprints when he spoke again, but he returned to our earlier subject. "For the last four days, I've picked up Sam by no later than five-fifteen, making sure we got home early enough to sit down together for dinner."

"That's great."

"My mother practically went into shock on Tuesday when I showed up. You'd have thought she wasn't used to seeing me in daylight."

I could tell he was going for self-deprecating humor, but it was revealing more than he probably intended. "How did your boss react to you leaving early?"

That he immediately stiffened suggested that all was not well at Heritage Hill Real Estate Development. "Clyde will just have to get used to it."

"Sam probably enjoyed having dinners with his dad." I managed not to mention my sadness for Sam that meals with his dad were the exception rather than the rule. No more unsolicited parenting advice from me. Once bitten, twice shy, and I'd already learned that when cornered, Luke could strike out, and his bites stung.

Luke turned to face me and lifted a quizzical brow. "Were you listening when I told you about all his tantrums this week?"

"He probably wanted to keep it a secret that he was happy to spend time with you," I said with a grin.

"That's probably it."

"Or maybe your cooking stinks."

"You're about to find out if that's true."

"Lucky me." And poor Luke. When he'd been on his best behavior, his son had been on his worst. "I'm sorry Sam's been throwing tantrums."

"It's not your fault. It's mine for giving in to his demands." He started for the stairs that led to the beach and motioned for me to follow.

"He's sure been a perfectly behaved sweetheart today," I said from behind him as we descended the steps.

Turning his head to the side, he answered, "Wouldn't you be sweet if you got your way." He blew out a frustrated breath. "Not all of us can be Dad-of-the-Year."

"You're a good dad, Luke."

He stopped so quickly at the bottom of the steps that I had to brace my hand on his back to keep from barreling into him. I tried to ignore the way the muscles in his shoulder bunched under my touch. My hand fell away as he turned back to me.

"You didn't have to say that."

His gaze was so intense, as if he was trying to determine if I really meant what I'd said. How could I not? And why would it matter so much to him what I thought?

"I didn't have to, but it's true. You love Sam. Anyone can see that."

His attention moved to the wavy-haired boy in question, who was using his shovel again to dig a gaping hole in the middle of the beach. Sam appeared too preoccupied with his project to notice us. A father's pride danced in Luke's expression. I wondered if there could ever be anything more attractive than a father's love for his child.

Together we started toward Sam. I caught Luke glancing sidelong at me.

"You probably see a lot of bad dads in your work."

"That's just it. Most of the time I *don't* see them. We work with a mostly at-risk student population, so many of the children in my caseload don't have a father present in the home."

We had reached the first pile of sand toys that were spread across the beach, so Luke crouched to collect them, but he tilted his head to the side to let me know he was still listening.

"So often, these dads leave the women in their lives behind to raise their children without even the benefit of child support." Even Alan hadn't deserted the mother of his child, but that still couldn't prevent him from being a loser in my mind.

"No wonder you were so worried about Sam when

I came late," he said as he stuffed two pails and a frog-shaped sand mold into a mesh bag.

At first I wondered if Luke had read my thoughts about my ex-husband, and I worried about just how skilled a mind reader he was, but he'd only responded to what I'd said aloud. That was just as well. It wouldn't be fair for him to be great with kids and animals and a mind reader, too. God just wouldn't give one person such an unfair wealth of skills, would he?

"Anybody can be a father," he said. "It takes a real man to be a dad."

His comment jerked me back from my journey of envy. I'd heard that saying many times, but it sounded so wise coming from Luke's lips. He was that real man he spoke of, in every way, and it was all I could do not to tell him so. That would be a conversation killer if I ever heard one. The conversation ended there, anyway, but without the strangeness my comment would have caused.

In the pair of beach sandals I'd bought earlier in the week as a gift to my poor, overheated feet, I traipsed over to where Sam was digging for new worlds beneath Mantua's rocky beach. Luke followed me, barefoot.

Sam looked up, for the first time noticing that we'd joined him on the beach. "When do we eat? I'm hungry."

"You ought to be," I told him. "The destruction of worlds can sure work up an appetite."

Sam tilted his head to the side. "What's an appetite?"

"It's your hungry belly," Luke told him, crouching down to tickle the spot he'd mentioned.

Sam burst into a round of giggles, slipping into his almost Sam-sized hole.

"We'll eat in about five minutes, so you need to shake the sand off and go wash your hands."

The boy crossed his arms in a stubborn stance. "I want to eat in my hole."

"Not going to happen, buddy. Food's up there." Luke pointed to the deck. "But after dinner, we can bury you in your hole if you want."

"Cool!"

Pout forgotten, Sam sprang from his burrow and scrambled toward the house.

"That went well," Luke said as he watched him go.

"You could have buried him right now if he threw another tantrum."

Luke looked at me as if I'd suddenly grown a dunce's cap or something. "Are you kidding? Sam is not getting buried unless he's good."

"Oh, it's a privilege then to get sand in the most uncomfortable places?"

"It is when you're four."

"Then I'm glad I'm not four anymore."

"I'm glad, too."

I turned to look at him, but Luke had already started toward the deck steps. What did he mean? That he was glad he wasn't a preschooler anymore or that I wasn't? And if he was glad *I* wasn't, then why?

I shouldn't ask; I knew that. Something told me it would be best for all involved—me in particular—if I just forgot about it. But for some reason I had to know what he was saying. What he was thinking. I just couldn't *not* know.

"Luke?"

The guarded look he gave me said more than his words likely would have. He was probably having as many second thoughts about what he'd said as I was over asking him about it.

Someone needed to look away so this awkwardness could pass, but I just couldn't do it. Luke didn't look away, either. Something strange and new fluttered in my chest. I didn't know how much time passed, only that I didn't want this feeling to stop and I wanted to keep looking at Luke.

The sound of pounding feet on wood brought both of us around. Above us, Sam stood at the deck rail, only the top of his head showing above the rail.

"Daddy. Daddy. Something smells like it's burning."

Chapter Eight

Hot dogs weren't so bad after all. At least, they were better than the steaks that looked like the charred contents of a burned-out building. Good thing Luke had the foresight to make extra filler dogs, or we might have been forced to dig into the two steak-shaped lumps of coal.

I still chuckled when I thought of our disappointing steak dinner, though Luke and I had long since cleaned the grill, loaded the dishwasher and buried Sam up to his chin in his hole.

Luke looked up from where he was using the last of the sky's light to build a fire in the beach pit. We'd promised Sam s'mores for dessert, so I balanced boxes of graham crackers and chocolate in my arms, with a bag of marshmallows perched on top.

"Are you laughing at my steaks again?" he asked, looking at me just as the first flames shot up from the newspaper and kindling.

"Maybe." I didn't bother trying to deny it since I'd been laughing sporadically about it all night.

"Hey, didn't my roasted potatoes and roasted corn make up for that one little mistake? Those turned out perfectly, even if Sam wouldn't eat them."

"More than made up for it." In fact, I'd had to restrain myself from eating the last of those crispy potatoes, spiced perfectly with olive oil, garlic and seasoned salt, right off Sam's plate. What had happened to my lack of appetite that had given me a figure like Popeye's Olive Oyl? If Luke cooked those for me every day, I'd probably look more like Brutus. "I was just craving steak."

"Fine, then. I owe you a steak." He used a big stick to stoke the fire.

Immediately, an image flicked against my cerebrum of Luke and me, alone across a candlelit table, with starched white napkins, crystal and china—the whole saccharine-sweet deal. I really was pitiful, wasn't I? Even my fantasies were clichéd. I might as well have pictured myself running across a field of daisies toward him or something. Again, a chuckle escaped, but it had nothing to do with grilling tragedies.

"Now quit the laughing or I'm going to start a marshmallow war."

"That's where you're mistaken." I paused long enough to set the crackers and chocolate aside and rip open the corner of the plastic bag in my hands. "You have to have artillery to make the first strike."

I started the battle myself, pelting him with the first two marshmallows.

Sam chose that moment to come running up to the fire pit. "Daddy, can we—" He stopped himself, looking shocked. "Miss Cassie's throwing marshmallows on the ground."

"I see that." Luke tsk-tsked. "She's not being very well behaved, is she?" He waited for Sam to shake his head before he added, "Do you think we should still let her have any s'mores?"

Sam seemed to consider for several seconds. "Maybe just one or two."

I grinned at him. "Thanks, Sam. How many are you planning to have?"

"Five."

Luke shook his head as he settled into the middle of the three lawn chairs we'd placed on one side of the fire pit. "Two. Max."

His son frowned, but he turned back to me. "Two."

I took the chair to Luke's right and started handing him marshmallows to put on one of the quadruple-pronged roasting tools we'd found in the garage. When our fingers brushed, mine tingled as if they'd been asleep and were just awakened by his touch. I shivered, not from the cold.

Luke misunderstood.

"Here." He pulled that same Michigan State sweatshirt he'd worn a few days before from the back of his chair, loosely draping it over my shoulders.

"Thanks," I managed, even though the musky scent of his cologne wafted through my nostrils.

Since I appeared to be the only one whose senses were being bombarded by our nearness, I busied myself, breaking the graham crackers in half and dividing the chocolate bars into cracker-sized pieces while he cooked. We became a perfect team with his heating the confections to a golden brown and my trapping the gooey mess between two crackers, with a chocolate squeezed in for good measure. Sam got to eat the first masterpiece.

"As soon as we're done and have this cleaned up, we have to get home," Luke told him right after he took the first bite.

"But Dad..." His full mouth gave his comment a garbled sound.

Luke shook his head to interrupt. "Tomorrow's Sunday. Church."

He said it with enough finality to discourage any further argument. Instead of trying right away, Sam took another big bite of his dessert. I wondered if Luke would mind if I interjected an argument of my own. I wanted the day to last a little longer, for the smiles and laughter to stretch through a few more hours and for those hours to slow.

As adorable as Sam was and as much as I enjoyed spending time with him, I realized that the person I wanted to spend those extended hours with was Luke.

Strange, I'd thought my scars were too deep, my wounds too permanent. But here it was before me. I still had the capacity to be interested in another man and to risk more of those wounds.

I didn't even have time to be unsettled by my realization because Sam chose that moment to present his own argument for more time.

"Can Miss Cassie come to church with us?"

Now I hadn't expected that. Nor had I really considered it. I already knew that all the Sheridans and the

Hudsons were members of the same small congregation, Lakeside Community Chapel. Aunt Eleanor had given me that information last week while trying to entice me into services.

A week ago, that had been at least one of my biggest deterrents. Was I ready to admit that Luke's presence anywhere would no longer keep me away, especially when my other excuses were gone now, as well? I opened my mouth to answer, still not sure what I would say, but Luke beat me to it.

"Sorry, buddy, but Miss Cassie doesn't go to church. Remember when I told you that some people don't go?"

"Why not?" Sam was looking at me, expecting me to explain something at a four-year-old level that I didn't know for sure myself.

Why not? I couldn't even say that I'd been mad at God for the destruction of my life. On some level, I'd always recognized that, like Sam and our sand castles, I was a key member of the demolition crew.

Sometimes I felt as if God had deserted me when I'd needed him most, but I understood now that I'd been the one to pull away. Maybe I'd always known that He wouldn't let me play the victim and would demand that I take my share of responsibility for the divorce. I wasn't ready then. Was I ready now?

"She doesn't have to tell us that, Sam. Some things are just private."

"Oh."

Just like before during the humiliating scene with the wedding party, Luke was stepping to my defense. His parents must have both passed on to him knight-inshining-armor genes because he couldn't help himself. But this time I didn't need it.

I cleared my throat. "I was just about to say that I haven't been to church for a while, but I've been thinking about going back. I'd love to go with the two of you tomorrow."

Only after I said it did I realize that I hadn't made sure Sam's invitation was okay with Luke. I turned to him with the question in my eyes.

"We'd love you to come with us." He didn't say more with words, but his gaze seemed to offer a personal invitation: *I'd love you to come with me.*

"We'll pick you up at nine."

"Nine?" I almost backed out right then. I'd spent most of the week not even rolling out of the sheets until nearly ten. Spiritual sustenance would come at the price of Z's. The soul was willing, but the lazy body was weak.

"We go to Sunday school, too," Sam explained.

"You do?" Apparently, I wasn't going to get the chance to test the water with my toe like I did at the lake's edge before I dived back into the whole church thing. "Of course you do," I added when Luke grinned.

I took a mental note to set my alarm before I went to bed. "I'll be ready."

And with a start I realized that when it came to returning to a formal practice of my faith in church, I already was.

"Cassie dear, we're so glad you could make it to services," Yvonne Sheridan told me as she gripped my hand between both of hers.

I'd barely made it out of my pew before she'd hurried over to me. "Did you see anyone you recognized?"

I chuckled at that. "About everyone looked familiar."

"Including Reverend Lewis?"

"Him most of all, but I kept wanting to peek behind the lectern to see if he was barefoot beneath his pastor's robe."

Yvonne's musical laughter filtered through the tiny sanctuary. "I assure you he wore shoes. He has a preference for wingtips."

As her son and grandson had followed me out of the pew and were standing next to me now, she stopped to greet both of them with kisses before turning back to me.

"So how did you happen to end up at Lakeside on this fine June morning?"

"Sam invited me."

Yvonne reached down and ruffled her grandson's hair. "Well, aren't you just a one-boy outreach program."

Luke leaned toward me and said conspiratorially, "Missionary and a demolition expert. What a combination."

Yvonne lifted a delicate brow in her son's direction, but he waved away her curiosity with a brush of his hand.

"You had to be there."

She nodded but wore the strange expression of someone trying not to smile. "So what do the three of you have planned today?" The grin did appear this time.

"Hadn't made any." Luke was regarding his mother with a cautious look.

"That's good. Neither have we."

Immediately, Luke's hand went up as if to ward off his mother's newest scheme, but Yvonne only laughed.

"Don't worry, sweetheart. I wasn't going to suggest an all-day board game marathon or anything."

Luke visibly relaxed, and I let out the breath I hadn't realized I was holding.

"It's such a lovely day that I thought Marcus and I could have a picnic with our grandson."

"A picnic!" Sam said it as though it might well be the first picnic in the history of civilization. "Can I go, Daddy?"

"I suppose."

"I'm going to go tell Papa," Sam said before hurrying out to the vestibule.

When he was gone, Luke turned his suspicious gaze back on his mother.

"What?" she asked innocently.

"Mother, what do you have up your sleeve now?"

"Nothing." She even looked offended. "I just thought it might also be a good day for you and Cassie to take Jack and Eleanor's boat out on the lake. The water's supposed to be really calm this afternoon. Waves are only one to three feet."

Luke nodded, not giving away anything he was thinking. This felt like a big dose of déjà vu, and the first match-up scene and rejection had been enough of a humiliation for one lifetime. I would have preferred to avoid seconds.

"No small-craft warnings?" he asked.

Small-craft warnings? Somehow I managed not to ask it out loud, but nothing could have prevented me from turning my head to look at him. Luke, though, kept his focus on his mother.

"Not unless something has changed since before Sunday school," she said.

"How big's the boat?"

"Just a twenty-four-footer. Big enough for an afternoon on the water but too small for travel."

"Where do they dock it?"

"There's an inlet about a half mile down the beach with a few slips in it."

What was going on? These two seemed to be talking from some parallel universe in which people discussed watercraft details rather than the matter at hand: Luke and I had just been set up on a date. I didn't care how big or where the boat was—as long as it was seaworthy of course. All I wanted to know was whether Luke wanted to go.

And then he turned to me. "Well, whatdya say, Cassie? Want to bob around in the water for a few hours?"

Thoughts of a forty-pound salmon returned with a vengeance. "When you say bob, you mean inside the boat, right?"

His grin made something tickle inside my belly. "If you insist."

"Then okay."

"Okay."

"Oh, good." Yvonne nearly rubbed her hands together in glee. She probably couldn't wait to get a call off to Europe. I could just imagine her running into the ladies' room and holding her cell phone above the stall door to get a signal.

After a few minutes of planning and directions regarding my aunt and uncle's boat, Luke and I headed out the church doors, minus Sam. Luke walked me to his car and opened and closed the door for me before crossing to the driver's side. It shouldn't have felt any different since he'd done the same thing that morning when they'd picked me up for church, but it was different. This was officially a date—my first real one since the divorce was final.

"Well, that was interesting," I said, once he was in the car.

"What do you mean?"

Although I'd spent enough time with Luke the last several days to be at ease in his presence, I started fidgeting, not certain what to do with my hands. Finally, I clasped them together on my knee. "If that wasn't a setup, then I don't know what one is."

"Mom sure thinks she's sly, doesn't she?"

I turned to look at him. "Why did you do it?"

"Do what?"

"Why did you let your mother coerce you into this...boat trip?" For the life of me, I couldn't bring myself to say *date*. At least by not doing so, I wouldn't have to graduate to the more telling term: charity date.

Luke's lips lifted. "You might not know me well enough to realize this about me, but I never do anything I don't want to do."

My breath caught. Was he saying what I thought he was saying?

But then he turned to face me and placed his hand atop my clasped ones. For a few seconds, I glanced down at our hands, my pulse racing.

When I looked up again, he was watching me, his expression having become serious. "I wanted to go."

I swallowed. My throat felt so dry. My palms, fortunately not touching his, were damp. The moment was too intense. My temptation was to take the coward's way out and look away, but I wouldn't allow myself to do it.

"Me, too."

Luke shifted into neutral and turned off the boat's ignition. Moving to portside—at least that's what I thought he'd called the left side—he lowered the anchor into the water where it caught and held.

Around us Michigan's blue-green waters shifted and swirled. Though the beach was still within sight, it was far enough that I wouldn't want to have to swim for it. Every few seconds, the beach repositioned itself in the distance as the boat rocked gently, tugging against its buried anchor.

Crouching low and dragging the life vest along with me, I moved to the L-shaped seating area near the stern of the boat.

"So this is what you meant by bobbing around?"

Luke joined me in the rear seating area. He was wearing a MSU cap, dark sunglasses and a white Michigan State T-shirt with a pair of swim trunks I recognized from the other day.

"Why, is your lunch coming for a return engagement?"

"No, I'm fine, I think." Maybe a little green around the gills, but I would survive. Anyway, I didn't want to see the bologna sandwiches and the cheese puffs we'd gobbled down for lunch again. Especially not the cheese puffs.

"The water always feels a little rougher when you're anchored. You have the knobs of your motion sickness wristbands on your pressure points, right?"

I held my arms wide so he could examine the positions of my bands.

"They look good." He brushed my wrists, making contact for the first time since that moment in the car, but the touch was brief.

"Give it a few minutes and see if you start to feel better. Keep your eyes on the horizon. If it doesn't help, we'll pull anchor in a few minutes."

I didn't hold high hopes of anything other than tilting my face up and being sea sick like a human Roman candle, but I stared at the navy-blue line where the water and the sky kissed and hoped for the best.

"So what did you think of church today?" he asked.

Because I recognized he was trying to distract me, I smiled weakly and tried to answer. "It wasn't too bad for a first time back in a while. At least Reverend Lewis preached on the 'Parable of the Talents' rather than something really tough."

"Don't worry. He was just taking a break after last week. He preached on Matthew 7, where Jesus talks about knowing His followers by the fruit they bear. You know. 'Every tree that does not bear good fruit is cut down and thrown into the fire.'"

Still wearing the jean shorts and loose T-shirt I'd thrown over my new royal-blue tankini, I sank down in the seat, leaning my head against the backrest and closing my eyes. The sun heated my face and created a warm, orange glow inside my eyelids. I could have pulled my sunglasses off the top of my head, but it seemed like too much effort.

"You okay?"

"Just relaxing." To convince him that I wasn't just waiting for the eruption to begin, I continued our conversation. "Maybe your minister took pity on me. That sermon would have been a rough one for a backslider to return to."

"Backslider? Nah. Just disillusioned after the divorce."

I weighed his words and then shrugged. "Probably."

How quickly he'd keyed in on something that had taken me years to figure out. Though I appreciated the fact that he didn't question me further, I still couldn't help asking, "How come you didn't ever question?"

"Who says I didn't? Or don't?"

My eyes opened. Luke's head was turned, and he was looking across the water and likely somewhere into the past. Settling my dark glasses in place over my eyes, I waited until he returned from those places for him to explain.

"After Nicole died, I kept taking Sam to church, but I started to question whether God really had a plan for our lives. Why would He allow my son to grow up without a mother when he'd already lived with parents who only tolerated each other? I never stopped believing that God created us, but I just didn't believe He was all that interested in what had happened to us since then."

Luke lifted his face skyward and then turned back to me. "In time, my anger cooled, and I changed my mind about most of those things."

"You went to church that whole time?"

"I just figured if I kept going through the motions of faith, I would feel something eventually. Healing takes time, but I haven't stopped believing."

"It does take time. We also have to *make* time to listen when God's talking."

He studied me for a few seconds. "You know this from experience?"

"God and I had quite a bit of time alone lately. We even worked out a few things."

One side of his mouth lifted, as he must have recognized that he was responsible for giving me so much free time. "I don't know whether I should apologize or say you're welcome."

"Neither."

His mischievous half grin spread to the other side of his mouth. I wished I could see behind those sunglasses because his eyes were probably twinkling, too.

As if he recognized my curiosity, Luke pulled his glasses low and looked at me over the top of them. "Do you need me to leave you alone on the beach a while longer? Because I can. We can dock now, and you'll still have most of the afternoon to pray and listen some more."

"No. I'm fine."

"Are you?"

"You mean…" I paused to touch my stomach. Luke had done it, I realized. He'd distracted me until the wave of nausea had passed. Either that, or those ridiculous bracelets with hard knobs on one side really did help prevent motion sickness, and I was pretty skeptical about that.

"Good," he said. "I didn't want to spend the day scrubbing out the boat."

"You could have told me to hang my head over the side."

He pointed his index finger as if to recognize my genius. "Good thinking."

"Remind me never to get sick around you because you'd make a lousy nurse."

I chuckled as I spoke the words, but my laughter died the minute I realized what I'd said: that Luke might be the one to care for me when I was sick. Worse than that, I'd implied that Luke and I had a someday. I stared down at the seat cushion, tracing my fingers along its rounded trim piece.

He'd removed his hat and glasses and was studying me when I finally looked up at him again. "You can't go and get uncomfortable being alone with me now. Ten minutes ago, you were all ready to toss your cookies in front of me."

His grin was contagious, and soon I was wondering what had ever made me feel so self-conscious.

"Are you recommending that I begin all my dates with a vomiting episode to ease the jitters?" Just saying the word jitters only compounded mine. I was on a real date with Luke Sheridan, and no matter how hard I tried to argue that we'd finally given in to our matchmakers' pressure, I was exactly where I wanted to be.

"Might work, but it will definitely cut down on the number of second dates."

With that, he lifted both hands to the tag of his T-shirt, and in one smooth movement, whipped it over his head. Tan with windblown hair, he'd never looked more ruggedly handsome. When he caught me watching him, he lifted one firm-looking shoulder and lowered it.

"It's hot out here. I don't know about you, but I'm going for a swim."

He didn't wait for an answer from me but stepped over the tiny latched door to the swim platform and dived into the water.

"How's the water?" I called out when he returned to the surface.

"It's amazing. You should come in."

Well, it was either that or stay there alone in the boat with no one to talk to, no one to distract me with conversation from the rock-rock-rock of the boat.

And it did tend to rock-rock-rock.

With motions far less fluid than his had been, I pulled off my T-shirt and shed my shorts and the motion sickness bands. Then I buckled myself into a life vest. Luke wasn't wearing one, but he appeared to be a stronger swimmer than I was. Also, there was no way I going to ruin my summer vacation, not to mention my first date in forever, by becoming another Lake Michigan drowning statistic.

I slipped out to the swim platform and stood there gathering my courage.

"Come on in. The water's fine."

"Here goes." I raised my arms and took a scissor leap into the blue.

The second my toes touched the water I wished I could scramble back into the air and right back on the boat. A squeal escaped me before the waves closed over my head. *Cold* did about as good a job describing this ice water as *forever* did at describing eternity.

Yes, the life vest had been a good idea since it only let me sink a few feet before pulling me back to the surface. I reemerged sputtering and flapping my arms. After several ineffectual strokes, I finally swam back to the platform and gripped its edge.

"Amazing?" I shrieked. "Fine? Are you kidding?"

It only took Luke a few long, smooth strokes to join me. "Maybe I should have said *brisk*."

"Maybe you should have."

"We could be grateful it's not as cold as Lake Superior."

"Believe me, I am."

"Well, now that you're in, you might as well enjoy the water." He pushed backward off the platform and did the backstroke for about twenty yards before turning to look at me. "Come on. Don't be a killjoy. You'd do it for Sam if he were here."

Though I figured I would have given even Sam a tough argument here, I pushed off after him. With a modified dog paddle, which was all I could manage with the life jacket, I finally reached the place where Luke was treading water. If I was going for the whole bathing beauty thing, I was falling a tad short.

"See, it's not so bad once you get used to it."

Though I suspected that my body was getting acclimated to the water by becoming numb, I nodded. What hadn't killed me was making me stronger.

For the next twenty minutes—probably less but it felt like more—we floated around in the water, playing chase games as if Sam had come with us all along. Luke tried to dunk me a few times, but my life vest gave me the upper hand, and he drank more than his share of lake water.

Finally, as he gripped the edge of the swim platform, he turned to me. "I don't know about you, but I'm getting cold."

I paddled up and gripped the platform next to him. "Really? I think it feels refreshing."

"Well, I guess we could stay in longer."

He paused to study my face. I didn't need to see his grin to know that my lips were blue. It was all I could do to keep my teeth from chattering out a rhythm that would make Carlos Santana proud.

"No, we don't have to do that. I'll get out just for you. I'm a real sacrificial gal that way."

"You definitely are." He reached over to brush back my hair, but I recognized his ulterior motive and shot back so that he dunked himself instead of me.

"Don't mess with a master," I warned when he surfaced again.

"I learned that lesson." He popped below the water and reemerged, smoothing his hair back from his face.

I expected him to be mad for that last indignity, but he was grinning as he swam up to me again. His smile warmed my skin, even in the frigid water. Who needed candlelight? Luke Sheridan could make even swimming in the freezing lake more fun than any date I could remember.

Luke climbed the platform ladder and stepped over to retrieve our beach towels. While I stood on the ladder waiting for him to return with mine, I glanced back at miles and miles of water. There wasn't a whale or even a forty-pound salmon anywhere in sight.

Chapter Nine

Now this was the life. Luke and I stretched out on the two loungers in the bow area in front of the cockpit, letting the sun evaporate the water droplets from our skin and remove the numbness from our limbs.

I had slipped back on the motion sickness bracelets, just in case they were the only things keeping my stomach from revolting. Shivering, I wondered how long it would be before my lips returned from blue to pink.

"Now this is the life," Luke breathed, his sunglasses propped on top of his head and his eyes closed.

"What?" he asked at my chuckle, but he still didn't open his eyes.

"Great minds just think alike."

He answered with one of those grunts that no longer bothered me the way they had when I first met him. Luke didn't waste words when a simple expression was enough.

I looked into the sky, taking in the frosted-blue backdrop with the cumulus clouds decorating it in cartoon shapes. Near the water's edge, a few seagulls floated and dived for snacks. After more than a week at the beach, I had concluded that those birds were annoying beach vermin, but here, from a distance, they looked regal. Part of God's creation. Part of God's plan.

I was still peering up at the sky when I breathed in the fresh scent of the water, letting my lungs hold it for a few seconds before exhaling.

"It's beautiful here, isn't it?" I said, some of my awe coming out in my voice.

"Yeah."

But when I glanced over, expecting him to say more, Luke had rolled to his side and wasn't looking at the sky at all. Or the beach. Or even the water.

He was looking at me.

My mouth went dry, and my cheeks heated, but his comment made me feel beautiful, whether he'd been talking about me or not. In case he wasn't, I didn't embarrass myself by thanking him. Bashfully, I looked up into the clouds again.

"A person could think about a lot of things while out here, surrounded by God's beauty," he said after a long time.

I made one of those affirmative grunting sounds myself, not even feeling the need to cover it with words.

"What discoveries did you make this week?"

His question surprised me. I almost asked him why he thought I'd made any discoveries, but then I remembered I'd already said that God and I had worked some things out together. Even if I hadn't said that, he could have guessed from the fact that I'd attended church that something had changed.

Before, I'd been glad that he hadn't pressed me to talk about it. I'd barely had the chance to digest it in the privacy of my own heart. But now I found that I needed to share it with someone, even if he had as many scars as I did. Probably more.

"That I was partly to blame for my divorce," I blurted, turning on my side the way he'd been before.

He was still resting just that way on the lounger across from me, but now he was looking at me skeptically. "So you forced him to cheat on you at gunpoint?"

I rolled my eyes. "No, not that way."

"Then how?"

"I agreed to the five-year plan."

"You agreed to let him cheat for five years?"

By now, I was smiling. "No. Forget the cheating part, okay?"

"Okay. So what was the five-year plan?"

"When I married Alan, he was ambitious and charismatic, a real go-getter. He had this plan of leaving the logistics company he worked for and building a company of his own in—"

"Let me guess. Five years."

I pointed to the tip of my nose to say he'd gotten the answer on the nose. "We were saving for that launch. Until we reached *our* goal of being financially secure, Alan thought we should delay starting a family."

His head propped on his hand, Luke seemed to consider. "Sounds like a reasonable plan…if you're into things like food and shelter and other frivolous nonessentials."

"Do you want to hear this or what?"

Suddenly becoming serious, he nodded.

"When I said 'financially secure,' what I really meant was 'well-off.'" I paused to let that settle before continuing. "After a few years, he starting hinting that he didn't want children at all, that our life together was perfect the way it was."

"Only it wasn't."

"No, it wasn't. That made it an even bigger slap in my face when he left me for a woman who was pregnant with his child. It wasn't that he didn't want kids. He just didn't want them…with me." I hated it that my voice cracked then. I hated it even more that it still mattered.

"You don't know that, Cassie." Luke shook his head adamantly. "He could have just played around and got caught."

I shrugged, but I wasn't ready to believe him.

"I'd thought you might have had fertility problems."

"We hadn't exactly…er…tested the system let's say when it came to the whole baby business." My cheeks and neck heated, and I had this infantile temptation to giggle, though nothing should have embarrassed me now. If I'd survived us discussing my ex-husband's infidelity, then I could live through this.

"Good. I felt lousy just thinking you might have had trouble, especially after I'd pointed out that you weren't even a parent and you were giving parenting advice."

"You were just fending off an attack."

"Well there's that," he said with a chuckle. "That didn't give me any excuse to be cruel."

"You don't have it in you to be cruel."

Though his eyes widened, Luke didn't try to argue

with me. "So tell me, how does this make you partly responsible for your divorce? If you were a prosecutor, I'd say you haven't made your case."

I sat up on the cushion and planted my feet on the boat deck in front of me, frustrated because he couldn't get it. "I said I agreed to the five-year plan. But that was just a symptom of having my priorities all out of whack. I wanted all of those things that money could buy."

Luke sat up and faced me. "Cassie, everybody wants things."

"But I'm such a classic overachiever. I was so ambitious, so driven that I married a man who was just like me—and all wrong for me. God had someone out there who was perfect for me, who would bring out the best in my character rather than the worst, but I wasn't listening."

"We've all been guilty of not listening. You just paid more than most."

"But it was more than choosing badly. After I was married, I didn't honor my husband or my marriage. I was so driven that I threw myself into my job one hundred percent. I even volunteered as a reading mentor after school. If my husband had actually come home from work once in a while, I still wouldn't have been there to spend time with him."

Luke shook his head, still refusing to buy my argument. How thickheaded could he be?

"Fine. You made a lousy choice, and then you made some mistakes. Those things happen. But you would have made changes to make your marriage work somehow. You didn't break your vows or jump ship."

I started to disagree again, but a sudden realization

had me clamping my mouth shut again. Maybe I was the thickheaded one here. I finally understood why he'd defended me. He was right: I would have stayed. Just as he would have stayed with Nicole, if given the chance. In that way, Luke knew me better than I knew myself.

"Thanks for saying that." I stared at my fingers, their tips still wrinkled from the water.

"And Cassie…" He waited until I lifted my gaze to his before he spoke again. "I told you before that your husband was a creep. But he was more than that. He was a fool not to recognize how amazing you are."

I swallowed. There had to be something I could say, but I had no idea what it was. I waited, half expecting him to add a punch line about what an amazing specimen of a neurotic I was or something. But he didn't. I didn't do it, either, though I would have given almost anything for some comic relief at that moment.

"Are you hungry?" Luke stood so quickly that the boat rocked. "I don't know about you, but I'm starving."

As usual, Luke was protecting me, even from the discomfort caused by his own words. I liked to think of myself as tough and independent, but I sensed that I could get used to always knowing someone—no one in particular, of course—was there to catch me.

"Swimming will do that to you."

"Hungry, too?"

"I could eat."

Our early dinner was another round of bologna sandwiches and cheese puffs from the cooler, but Luke made it well-rounded this time by adding baby carrots.

"Almost a whole meal in orange. Is that lucky or what?" I said once we'd settled back into our seats and were floating and eating casually.

"If we had some food coloring, we could have transformed the sandwiches, too."

"Orange bologna, yum."

He pulled his cap low over his eyes to shade them from the sun. Its MSU insignia caught my interest and renewed some of my lingering questions over Luke's past.

"Tell me about Michigan State."

My question must have surprised him because he stopped with his sandwich only a few inches from his mouth and then lowered it back on the plate without taking a bite. "I told you it was Nicole's alma mater. I just passed through there."

I pointed to his T-shirt he'd put back on and then to the hat. "You wear MSU stuff all the time."

He stared down at his T-shirt before looking up again. "Why do you care? You're not a U of M fan, are you?"

His look of horror made both of us laugh. The arch rivalry between the two universities was legendary.

Finally, he lifted his hands in surrender.

"Okay. Okay. Nearly every Christmas, birthday, Valetine's Day and anniversary, Nicole bought me Michigan State stuff, so about half my wardrobe would work well at any fraternity house on campus. I guess she wanted to remind me of our shared past."

My guess was that his wife had wanted to remind him of something else entirely: his lack of a college diploma. My unflattering thoughts of the dead must have shown in my expression because Luke hurried on with his story.

"I'm a guy. What can I say? If it's clean and it doesn't have any major holes, then I'm still wearing it."

"You never told me what you studied. Or why you didn't finish."

Luke shrugged but straightened in his seat, setting his plate aside. "I tried on college for a few years, but it just never fit right. I studied business, but I hated talking about problems when I could be using my own two hands to fix them. That's why things work so well between Clyde and me. He trusts me to take care of the problems *and* get my hands dirty. Clyde knows I can handle it."

Luke's last comment punctuated everything else he'd said. *Clyde knows I can handle it.* Luke might as well have said, "Clyde believes in me." I could understand why his boss would. What I couldn't understand was that there ever had been someone who didn't believe in him.

"How did Nicole feel about you taking a different path instead of higher education?" I knew it was a loaded question, and yet I couldn't keep myself from asking it.

"I told you I was always a disappointment." He flicked a glance my way and then looked away when he saw my stark reaction. "Now don't blame Nicole. It wasn't what she'd signed on for. When I dropped out, she thought I was only taking a break. That I would go back and finish what I started. She thought I was a failure for not doing it."

"How could she even think that? You are not, have never been and could never be—"

He held up his hand for me to stop before I could get out the words *a failure.* I might not have said them anyway. Luke and those words didn't belong in the same sentence.

"Did I ever tell you how she died?"

"A car accident."

"Did I tell you what happened right before?" His voice sounded strange.

I shook my head, dread pulling on my heart like icy fingers. I had the feeling I wouldn't want to hear whatever he was about to say.

"We were arguing. I don't even remember about what. We bickered about everything by that time. She decided to take a drive, just to cool off. She ended up dead instead."

"Oh Luke..." So much made sense right then—the many little things Luke had said, so much of his pain. "It wasn't your fault."

"I let her get in the car."

Years of his guilt could be summed up in that sentence. It was simple and yet complicated, tied in an intricate web of half-truths that were more painful than lies.

"It was an accident, Luke. The police said she ran a stop sign, and a car hit her broadside."

He looked up at me from the deck, his confusion apparent.

"My aunt told me."

"Oh." He appeared to think for a moment, and then his jaw tightened. "Did she also tell you the police said after I admitted that we'd been arguing that I shouldn't have allowed her to drive so upset?"

"No, but it wouldn't have changed my opinion." I said it as if he should have cared what I thought when his opinion was the only one that mattered. And his was killing him.

There had to be some way for me to help him see the truth, to help him see what I saw when I looked at him. Someone good. Someone strong. And someone who would never intentionally hurt anyone. But I sensed I needed to start from a neutral place—a place we'd once walked together—if I wanted him to hear me at all.

"I can't get over what a funny pair we are," I said, waiting for him to look up at me again before I continued. "Just a regular cheesy poster advertising weddings and happily ever after. You in your tiny tux and me in scratchy periwinkle."

"Is that what they called that ugly purpleish-blue?" he asked, his hard expression softening.

"That's it."

"Are you saying we missed our calling to write greeting card poetry?"

"Maybe."

"I don't think we'd sell many cards."

"Oh, I would. I'm an overachiever, remember?"

"I forgot."

I paused, needing to find a smooth segue into the subject that really mattered, but there wasn't one. Still, it had to be said. "Doesn't it get exhausting?"

"What?"

"Carrying around all that guilt with you on top of that chip you already have on your shoulder."

When he turned to plant his feet on the deck and

crossed his arms, I realized I could have started off more gently. Just another reminder that diplomacy wasn't my strong suit.

"Listen, you keep beating yourself up for something that wasn't even your fault. When you're not doing that, you're killing yourself trying to prove you're not a failure when the only person who ever thought so isn't here to see it."

I should have stopped there. I was in way over my head, and I knew it. Hadn't I learned my lesson the first time when I'd nosed into Luke's business and he'd all but told me to take my advice and shove it?

It would be easier to just back down, to find some way to smooth over this conversation and make nice before Luke pulled anchor and dropped me back at the beach. But I'd spent a lifetime trying not to make waves, and here I was rocking the boat…literally.

Come to think of it, I'd been different with Luke from the beginning, more invested, even when I'd had no right to be. I still didn't have the right, but the words burned inside me. Maybe I needed to say them as much as he needed to hear them.

"Don't you see it, Luke? You're not lacking something. You never were. You're wonderful just the way you are."

His arms still crossed, Luke started shaking his head, as if he was unwilling to hear what I had to say. Why couldn't he see what I saw, what probably everyone saw except for the one woman who'd promised to love and honor him for life?

"It was Nicole who couldn't see it," I said before I could stop myself. "You're an amazing father and a strong, caring man. You're even a man of faith who has the courage to admit you still question."

He leaned forward now, elbows on his knees and his hands gripped together, but he was still shaking his head. "You're wrong about me, Cassie. I'm none of those things."

"You're all of those things. I see it. And she was a fool not to."

Once the words were out of my mouth, my breath hitched. The cat was so out of the bag, and there wasn't any easy way to shove it in again. It was so close to what he'd said to me, and I still figured his comment was three-quarters pity and one-quarter his just being a nice guy.

Worse yet, in the fervor of my speech, I'd planted my feet on the deck and faced him, leaning closer so that now no more than a foot separated us.

For several seconds, neither of us spoke. We didn't move, either, if you didn't count the way I was wringing my hands together as if one just might squeeze the life out of the other.

I could only imagine what he saw when he looked at me. I had to be humiliation personified. No one else needed to let him know about my growing feelings for him when I'd just gone and outed myself. Luke only looked bewildered, as if he'd like to believe what I'd said but couldn't take the leap.

I started to pull away, going for any exit when a graceful one hadn't been possible since I'd said, "I see it." Probably long before. But Luke reached for my hands, taking them sweetly in his. Luke's hands were warm and strong and roughened by honest work.

That same tingly sensation I remembered from when we'd brushed hands the night of my aunt's wedding party spread in my fingertips, but I felt more than that. There was a warm constancy to his touch, and I felt the rightness in our gentle connection.

Maybe Luke felt the same pull that I did, the need for closeness that I'd sensed from the moment we'd met for the first time as adults.

Would his arms make me feel as safe as his hands already had? Would I finally be able to sink into a man's arms and feel certain that he would catch me if I fell? I waited, hoping he would draw me near.

Luke didn't move. "Thank you" was all he said.

I blinked and shook my head to get my bearings straight. Had I misread this whole situation? Had he just reached out to me in gratitude for my kindness and I'd manufactured a romantic scenario out of that simple gesture?

Now I was really humiliated. I needed to rock the boat, all right. Hard. So I could fall overboard and let the water swallow me with one freshwater gulp.

"What is it?" Luke was looking at me strangely. "Don't you want me to kiss you, Cassie?"

What? I cleared my throat. "No...I mean yes...I mean no, I do." Frustrated, I shook my head. "How am I supposed to answer a question like that?" How was I supposed to say anything at all with my heart staging its own Indianapolis 500 and my hands creating a second Lake Michigan? I started to pull my damp hands free, but he pressed his thumbs into my palms and kept holding on to me.

Luke's eyes were smiling before the expression moved to his mouth. "How about I pose it like I would have when we first met? Do you want to kiss me? Yes or no. Circle one."

"Sorry, don't have a pencil right now, but yes."

"I guess that will have to do." Tugging gently on both of my hands, he pulled me forward until our heads were but a breath away. He paused for a heartbeat, or a thousand of them, and then covered my lips with his own.

Luke's kiss wasn't a dance of lips, vying for angle and tension. His lips merely sank into the cushioning of mine, and he remained there, warm and deeply present, as seconds ticked by. He tasted like cheese puffs and sunshine.

I had the oddest sensation of coming home, which didn't make sense because my apartment was more than two hundred miles away.

This was the same boy I'd kissed under the table at my aunt and uncle's wedding before I knew how precious and personal such a touch could be, the depth of emotion it could convey. This was the same man who'd told me he wasn't interested in dating anyone, let alone me. And this was the one man to whom I was in grave danger of losing my heart.

When he withdrew his head, he pressed his cheek against mine.

"What took you so long?" I breathed before my good sense returned. Just a first kiss, and already I was sounding like a demanding girlfriend.

His chuckle rumbled against my cheekbone. "Sorry. I was working up my courage."

I pulled back and looked into his eyes to see if he was serious. "With me of all people."

"You especially. You were the first girl I ever kissed."

"Well, I would sure hope so unless you were scouring your preschool for dates."

"Well…" The twinkle of confidence had returned to Luke's gaze, the spark that I hoped he would never lose again no matter what happened in the future.

I shook my head, trying to look disappointed. "And I thought I was special. I carried a basket of flowers and everything. I should have known."

All the playfulness fled from his gaze, and his eyes darkened. "You do know, right? You're incredibly special." Even as he said it, he lifted his hand and brushed his thumb across my lower lip. "So special."

I couldn't help leaning in to the sweetness of his touch. So this was what it felt like to be cherished. I could get used to it if he kept touching me that way. Luke leaned so close that I could feel his warm breath feather across my mouth.

"I haven't touched anyone like this in…a long time," he whispered.

"Me, neither," I answered, though I understood that he was talking about since his wife died. So much pain and guilt had to have been enfolded in that comment, and I wished I could help him to toss it away once and for all.

"I haven't wanted to until now."

"I'm glad," I managed to get past the lump in my throat.

"So you really did want to spend time with me?"

Since I'd been closing my eyelids in a huge hint that I wouldn't mind being kissed again, my eyes fluttered open. "What?" I cleared my throat as I leaned back in the seat. "What are you saying?"

His chuckle baffled me as much as his question. A lifetime of insecurities filtered through my thoughts. Finally, he took mercy on me and answered.

"Do you know how lousy a person can feel when he's jealous of his own son?"

"Why would you be jealous of Sam?"

"Because of you."

"You're kidding, right?" But even as I asked it, I sensed that he wasn't.

"He is a pretty cute kid. And it wouldn't be the first time a woman has hung around a guy to be with his kid."

Only because he was a miniature replica of his daddy, I wanted to say but didn't. I was a chicken to the core. Still, I had to make my interest in Luke clear to him.

"I guess I did like Sam better at first." I shook my index finger at him. "You weren't exactly nice to me the night of the rehearsal dinner."

"And now?"

"You've been very nice to me lately."

"You know what I meant," he said with frown.

I nodded because I did. "Now," I repeated, my pulse sprinting. Could I say it? Was I brave enough to risk everything by telling him the truth? Probably not, but I decided to fake it. "Now I still think Sam is great, but I'm pretty crazy about his dad."

Luke stared at me for several seconds, making me wonder if I should have done us both a favor and kept my feelings to myself.

Then, without preamble, Luke leaned across the aisle, slanted his lips across mine and kissed me again and again, his fingers curling into the hair at my crown. The moment I was over my surprise, I was kissing him back with just as much intensity, my hands clasped at the back of his neck.

I felt so precious in Luke's arms, so valued. I had this heady understanding that at least one man didn't think of me as second best.

When he finally pulled slightly away and pressed his forehead to mine, I was embarrassed to be out of breath. His breathing wasn't exactly regular, either.

"That was nice," he whispered.

"A little too nice."

"Maybe."

As if we'd timed our movements, we both pulled back then, retreating to our opposite sides of the boat and glancing around us. Somehow I hadn't noticed it before, but we were the only boat anchored in view of this stretch of shoreline, and though it was an incredibly beautiful June day, this part of the beach was deserted. Our boat appeared to be encapsulated by water and sky and sand.

We were alone. Too alone for a couple as attracted to each other as we were. Neither of us were innocents; we'd both been married before. And we'd both been lonely for a long time. We needed to take hold of our good sense before this situation got out of hand.

Just as I started turning back Luke's way, I sensed movement to my right. The boat dipped as he climbed through the door in the windshield and started pulling back in the anchor. When he sensed my gaze on him, he turned back to me.

"It's time for us to get back," he said.

"Probably."

A grin pulled at his lips. "No, absolutely."

I nodded. "Sam has to be missing you, anyway."

He laughed at that. "You're joking, right? Mom has probably been plying him with ice cream and candy all afternoon, and she'll give him back to me in a sugar haze."

"She wouldn't do that, would she?"

Luke seemed to consider for a few seconds before he grinned and shook his head. "She's usually more worried about his teeth than I am."

He turned his attention to pulling the anchor over the side of the boat. Immediately, the rocking that had come from the boat pulling against its anchor transformed to the gentle sway of the waves themselves.

As he climbed into the cockpit, he looked back at me again. "Besides, she wouldn't want to do anything to mess up her matchmaking scheme."

"She and Aunt Eleanor have worked too hard at it to ruin their plans now," I agreed, relieved he'd chosen another safe topic. He seemed as reluctant as I was to discuss the physical awareness between us that seemed to have surprised him as much as it had me.

Luke started up the boat again though he allowed it to idle until I'd moved through the windshield door and had taken the seat next to him.

Luke glanced back at me over his shoulder. "Cassie, I don't want to do anything to mess this up, either."

Chapter Ten

I awoke to the sounds of thunder early Monday morning, but even a storm couldn't dampen my sunny outlook. This wasn't California, after all. I had to expect a little rain to fall here sooner or later, and I'd seen nothing but sunshine since I'd arrived.

Besides, Mom had always said that if I didn't like the Michigan weather, I needed to wait fifteen minutes for it to change. On that at least, Mom had always been right. I could remember times in my childhood when we'd seen sunshine and rain and snow, all on the same day.

Climbing out of bed, I padded to the window and glanced out at the dark, angry sky. Since my window was at the front of the house, I couldn't see the water, but I guessed that it was just as dark and just as furious. I expected to see all kinds of nasty weather today, possibly even a water funnel coming off the lake. Even if my salvation was sure so I was technically ready to die, I wasn't a big fan of the idea this morning.

Especially not after my wonderful Sunday with

Luke. That was selfish, and I knew it, just as it was more than a little self-serving for me to hope that God hadn't scheduled Jesus's Second Coming for today, when this thing between Luke and me was still so new.

With so many Christians in the world—so many births, graduations, wedding days and budding romances—God could hardly work around everybody's schedules. I realized that, but that still didn't keep me from hoping this day wasn't *the* day.

On the likely chance that it wasn't, I put on my slippers, preparing to go down and feed Princess. She would be disappointed that it was me feeding her instead of her hero Luke, who'd fed her dinner last night before he left, but she was just going to have to deal with it.

Thirteen days and count—

I stopped myself. Who was I kidding? I no longer wanted to count the days until I could leave this place. That would mean leaving Luke and Sam. I couldn't help smiling as the perfect day Luke and I had spent together seeped into my thoughts. My heart warmed over the laughter and deep conversations we'd shared. My cheeks heated when my thoughts turned to the kisses.

I didn't even have to wonder when I would see him next. He'd phoned last night just as I'd crawled into bed to invite me on a dinnertime fast-food picnic tonight at the park. That same jolt of excitement I'd felt when Luke's rich baritone voice had come through the telephone line filled me again.

Did he think if he waited until this morning to call

that I'd be all booked up? I laughed out loud at that as I descended the steps. I didn't know anyone in Mantua who didn't attend Lakeside Community Chapel, and the selection of single men younger than sixty at the church was limited at best.

"Yes, offers are just coming out of the walls," I said aloud since no one was there to contradict me.

There was only one offer that I was interested in, anyway, and today that meant chowing on burgers and fries and waiting for the first ant to arrive at the picnic.

It was Luke who'd suggested that we plan something with Sam this time. With as much giddy anticipation as I was feeling though our date was still hours away, I figured his idea was a good one. We needed a chaperone.

The silly image of a four-year-old chaperone and his two thirty-year-old charges made me smile again. How I was going to be able to fill my day until our date I didn't know. I hadn't been this excited for a date since…well never.

From the cabinet I retrieved a can of salmon delight cat food and stood over the sink to open the pop-top lid. I made that clicking noise in my mouth, just as I'd heard Luke do. I didn't know why I bothered. Just because it had worked for him didn't mean Princess would deign to take pity on me.

It didn't matter, anyway. She was eating, drinking and visiting her litter box on a regular basis, so everything was fine. I'd fulfilled my obligations to humans and felines, even if Princess and I hadn't become the great friends Aunt Eleanor expected we would.

"Here kit-kit-kit," I called out of habit, knowing full well she wouldn't come.

Even if she didn't, Princess wasn't all bad. I might not have been her favorite person, but she had yet to put a single scratch on me, even when I'd been asleep and probably a tempting target. I wasn't ready to say she was a real *princess* or anything, but maybe I'd exaggerated her murderous tendencies the teeniest bit.

Only thirteen more days and my aunt and uncle would be returning from their trip to care for their little darling. They would expect me to go home when they did. I couldn't break my promise to Uncle Jack and be the houseguest who wouldn't leave, either.

But I didn't want to leave. Not yet.

Luke had said he didn't want to do anything to *mess this up* between us. I understood that he'd been talking at least in part about physical intimacy, but had he meant more than that? What was the "this" between us? Was it something worth pursuing?

I stopped myself before my crazy imagination could travel any further. Was I really thinking of something as outrageous as a future between Luke and me? Beyond being too soon to consider such a thing, I understood it wasn't possible. I had my life in Toledo, my job, my students and my friends. Luke had just as much here in Mantua. He had a job where he felt valued and a home near his parents so he had loving child care for Sam.

This thing between us had mistake written all over it. It had an expiration date as clear as is printed on a gallon of milk and a lot more final. Even the milk had a few days of life beyond the final sale date.

Thirteen days and holding.

Something brushed my ankle then, and I let out a yelp before I could stop myself. At my feet was none other than Princess herself, looking up at me with intense green eyes. If my outburst had frightened her at all, she didn't show it but only meowed pitiably and started weaving in and out between my legs the way she'd done to Luke.

"Now you decide to come to me, you silly girl." Briefly, I considered bending to pet her or turning on the faucet for her but decided against both. That would be too much too soon, and as Luke had recommended, I didn't want to seem too desperate. Princess would only run away, and we'd be back to square one.

The cat stopped to eye me again and then continued weaving figure eights, her soft fur tickling my ankles. I couldn't believe it. What had happened to the hissing, spitting monster that had been alone with me in the house for more than a week?

Again, she meowed as if she'd lost her best friend.

"I suppose you're wanting your breakfast."

I emptied the can of food into her special bowl and set it on her place mat. She sauntered over for one of her sniff-and-ignore sessions, but when she reached the bowl, she dug in. I couldn't believe my eyes.

"Boy, you were hungry, weren't you? Does that taste pretty good?" I crooned.

I would have turned a cartwheel right then and there, that is if I'd ever been able to do a cartwheel that didn't end up as a splat on the floor. This wasn't a major accomplishment; I realized that. Cats ate when they were hungry. But after all this time Princess had chosen to eat for me.

Was it because she finally realized I wasn't going anywhere—for now—and she'd just better get used to me? Funny, I sensed that wasn't it, that instead she was taking pity on me.

I would have dismissed the thought for the ridiculous notion it was, but Luke's image popped into my head again. I was in a vulnerable place with Luke Sheridan. This could only end badly. People were going to get hurt when it did.

I was on shaky ground, and I knew it. If I didn't know better I would say that Princess knew it, too.

The last Wednesday before I was to leave Mantua, I had just settled back for another one of those amazing afternoon naps on my aunt and uncle's deck lounger when the phone rang. Without getting up I reached for the portable handset on the table next to me alongside the lidded cup of lemonade, spray bottle filled with water, an individually packaged snack bar, bug spray and a container of sunscreen.

I was nothing if not Johnny-on-the-spot prepared with my table of provisions after more than two weeks of good practice. It took preparation to make sure a good beach bum afternoon wasn't spoiled by the need to go in too soon.

"Hudson residence, Cassie speaking," I said into the receiver, not jumping to any conclusions about who would be on the other end. Lately, the caller was just as likely to be Luke as my aunt. More likely. At least once every day, he called to make plans for that evening, and every night after he went home, he would phone just to say good-night. Sometimes he phoned for no reason at all in the middle of the day. A woman could get used to that kind of attention.

"Cassie, it's so good to hear your voice."

"Uncle Jack?" My uncle's voice had me springing up in my seat. "Has something happened to Aunt Eleanor?"

"Of course not. Why would you think that?"

Uh, because you haven't liked to talk on the phone in all the years I've known you, I somehow managed not to say. "I just usually talk to Aunt Eleanor."

"She's just...ah...busy."

At first, I thought my uncle sounded strange. Then the thought struck me that if Uncle Jack was calling, he just wanted to be in charge of flight details. *Return flight details.* I'd been hiding from it for as long as I could, but here was proof that my time with Luke was running out, and there wasn't a thing I could do to stop it.

Four days and holding.

But since no matter how hard I held on, time wasn't going to stop for me, I braced my hand on the lounger's armrest and prepared to learn the information I didn't want to hear.

"Will you need me to pick you up at the airport Sunday, or do you have a ride?"

He didn't answer immediately, but I could hear muffled voices as if he'd covered the phone. "You know, I was thinking that...ah...your aunt and I haven't really had the chance to do Paris up right."

I frowned into the phone. "What?"

He cleared his throat. "You know, we haven't even

had the chance to see the Mona Lycee at the Loo and the Champs of Lisa yet."

I couldn't help laughing, though I still couldn't understand what he was getting at. "You mean the 'Mona Lisa' at the Louvre and the Champs d' Elysée, right?"

"Yeah, sure."

He coughed, making me wonder if he was getting sick from all that European air.

"Anyway," he began, "we were thinking about extending our trip a bit."

My chest tightened, and suddenly I was the one having trouble getting an answer out. "How long were you thinking?"

"Not much. Just another two weeks. But only if it's okay with you to stay a little longer."

"Oh no. I don't think that will be a problem."

When the line went quiet, I realized I'd responded too soon, been too anxious to take them up on their offer.

"I wouldn't want you two to miss any of the sights while you're in Paris," I hurried on to cover the awkward silence. "Like the Louvre."

"Oh, good, I'm sure we'll have time to see all the rest of the sights by then," he told me.

Come to think of it, how could anyone have spent three weeks in Paris and not made it to one of the most famous museums in the world? I'd been had again and this time by my uncle, but I knew who'd put him up to it.

"So is Aunt Eleanor still…ah…busy?" I had a good

idea what she'd been busy doing before: egging my uncle on in the newest chapter of this matchmaking scheme.

"No, she's...uh...done now." In another rustle of movement and voices, he handed my aunt the phone.

"Hello, sweetie. How's my girl?"

"Which one?" I asked, repeating the same tired joke we'd shared nearly every time she'd called.

"The human one."

"She's good."

"Then how's my kitty."

I was tempted to tell her that Princess had eaten the neighbor's parakeet and had been on the lam for two days, but right now I was too curious what my aunt would say once we got past the preliminaries. "She's fine."

The fact was Princess and I were getting on pretty well now. She came right out whenever I popped open a can of food and ate most of it without any complaint. Or rather not many complaints—she was a cat after all, and finicky was built into her DNA.

Occasionally, she even rubbed up against my calves when she thought it might hurry up her dinner. She still hadn't chosen to drink from the faucet for me, and petting her was out of the question, but the kitty had her standards, and I could live with that.

"My Jack tells me you're going to stay a little longer for us. Thanks so much for that."

"Not a problem," I answered though I should have been thanking her.

"We'll come back on Friday the seventh, but we want you to stay at least until Sunday the ninth, so we can spend some time with you."

Two extra weeks—it wasn't forever, but it was something. Still, I was dying to know where this most recent development had originated. "Have you talked to Yvonne lately?"

Aunt Eleanor laughed into the phone. "She's my best friend. I talk to her all the time. Why do you ask?"

I answered her question with a question. "What'd she tell you?"

"Let me see…that the west Michigan weather has been beautiful. That she misses us terribly."

My aunt stopped when I cleared my throat. I didn't need to clarify what I was really asking, but she gave an answer I wasn't expecting.

"She said she saw you in church. Twice."

"That's right. I've been thinking about a lot of things since coming here."

"It is a great place for meditating."

I murmured an agreement, closing my eyes and breathing the place in once again.

"Yvonne also said that you and Luke have found each other."

Because she couldn't have put it more succinctly, all I could answer was "oh." I didn't have to acknowledge it because she already knew it was true. It had happened with a lot of pushing and shoving from Aunt Eleanor and from Yvonne, not to mention Sam's cajoling, but that couldn't change the truth that we'd found each other.

Or the truth that I'd have to leave soon. Every hour that Luke, Sam and I spent together seemed even sweeter because it could only be temporary. Colors were more intense. Aromas, headier. Each moment was a potential memory, and I found myself hoarding all of them. Even this two-week reprieve was just delaying the inevitable.

"You're not happy?" Eleanor asked after a long pause.

I let out a long breath. "I don't know. It's probably such a mistake. Don't get me wrong. Luke's great. But there can't be any future—"

"How do you know what the future holds?"

"I don't but..." I let my words fall away. Until she interrupted me with the question, I didn't realize that I'd mentioned the future or that I'd given away my secret wish that there might be one for Luke and me.

"You're going to have to learn to trust and wait, sweetheart. God will help you figure it all out."

"I'll try," I told her. I wondered if she realized what a tough assignment she'd just given me. Trust had never come easily for me, and after all I'd lived through, I'd sworn off it completely for my own health. But God and I were beginning to have an understanding, and I would try.

"While you're meditating out there, why don't you try reading Proverbs chapter three verses five and six?"

I couldn't help chuckling. Aunt Eleanor had always loved trying to come up with a Scripture to match every situation. I wondered if she'd been madly flipping through a concordance for appropriate verses even as we spoke.

"I will."

As soon as we ended the call, I got up from my chair and returned to the house. Apparently, my table of provisions wasn't complete because I didn't have a Bible out there with me. I hadn't even packed one when I'd left Ohio, so I went on a hunt for one. I hit the mother lode in the great room's built-in bookshelves: New International Version, New American Standard, Revised Standard and King James, even a copy of The New Oxford Annotated Bible that looked intimidatingly like a textbook.

Not a regular enough Bible student to have a preference, I grabbed one with a pretty brown leather cover, fumbled my way to Proverbs, located the third chapter and started reading. "Trust in the Lord with all your heart, and do not rely on your own insight. In all your ways acknowledge him, and he will make straight your paths."

I had to hand it to Aunt Eleanor. She had chosen well this time. She made it sound so easy, this trusting business. If it were so easy, then why did I feel as if I was jumping off a cliff into the unknown?

It was all I could do not to start skipping as the three of us walked along Mantua's tiny boardwalk later that night. Not four days anymore but eighteen. I knew that eighteen would eventually be four again and then three and two, but I didn't want to think about that now, not when we were surrounded by the sounds of laughter and carnival games and the strong and competing smells of Polish sausage sandwiches and deep-fried elephant ears.

Though it was still early, colorful lights flashed around us from the Ferris wheel and the Scrambler to the sprinkling of carnival games. This was no Cedar Point. It was even a far cry from the smaller Michigan's

Adventure Amusement Park in Muskegon. Still, Sam shook with excitement. I knew just how he felt.

"Can we ride all the rides, Daddy?"

Luke looked one way and then the other, scanning the five or so rides that would be appropriate for a four-year-old, before glancing at me mischievously. "We sure can. You can ride them all twice."

"Boy, Sam, you're sure lucky. Your daddy's really generous."

"Look, there's tickets." Sam shot off toward the booth that already had half a dozen people in line.

"I guess we need some tickets." Luke started after him and then stopped, turning back and extending his hand my way. I was reading too much into it, but it felt as if he was truly reaching out to me. Offering more than friendship. Offering....

Though I was kind of expecting one of those open arms greetings—not quite with a field of daisies but close—I got a rude awaking the moment his fingers closed over mine. He took off at a jog, dragging me like a weighted rag doll behind him.

I was convinced I would cough up a lung or two before we finished the fifty-yard dash to the ticket booth. Maybe I should have spent less time admiring the beach in front of my aunt's house and more time running on it.

"Here, Daddy, I'm up here." Sam waved madly, though there were only two people separating us from his place in line. Those two waved us up to where he was.

"You're not asthmatic, are you?"

Listening to my labored breathing, I couldn't imagine why he'd asked. "Don't you think you should have asked me that before you dragged me across the boardwalk?"

"You're not, are you?"

I shook my head. "Good thing for you I'm just amazingly out of shape."

He pulled our joined hands wide so that I came around to face him. His gaze lowered from the filmy, cap-sleeved blouse I had tied at the waist over an orange tank top to my faded jeans shorts to my no-back sneakers and then back up to my face.

"I think you're in great shape."

I was about to get all flustered and red until the next comment came out of his mouth.

"You've gained some weight since you've been here—"

"What did you say?" I yanked my hand from his.

Luke had glanced at the front of the line, but now he looked back to me, a slow smile spreading. "You didn't let me finish. I was going to tell you how much healthier you look now. How much prettier. That first night you looked so pale and underfed I wondered if you were okay."

"Did I ever tell you how much your effusive compliments embarrass me?"

"I said you looked prettier now."

"That's true, but I doubt anything you said would read well in lines of poetry."

"What I'm feeling just might."

I just stared at him. I would have asked him what he meant, if we hadn't reached the front of the line right then. Luke pulled his wallet from his pocket and plunked down enough money for an all-rides bracelet. By the time Sam was done tonight, even he would probably be sick of the motorcycles, race cars, boats and carousel horses.

After the string bracelet with its metal tab was clipped around his wrist, Sam grabbed both of our hands and pulled us to his first-choice ride. It was the motorcycles, of course. Should I have guessed anything different?

Luke directed Sam to the entrance in the circular fence surrounding the ride, and we both waved to him as he climbed aboard a metallic blue motorcycle. The chopper-style cycle was paired with another of lime-green in a bike rally that ran in circles but never reached a destination.

As the ride started and Sam and four other boys and girls two-wheeled along, blaring horns and waving all the while, a lump formed in my throat. Was this what it would be like if Luke, Sam and I stayed together forever? No, I couldn't think about that, couldn't dull the brightness tonight by asking for more than was possible.

Still, I was dying to know what Luke meant by his comment. That he loved me? Or that lines of verse could be written as an ode to my beauty? *What I'm feeling might.* I shouldn't ask, yet I had to know. I would come out of my skin tonight if I didn't.

When I turned back to him, I caught him watching me again, his expression so stark and unguarded that my hand might have reached up to touch his face if I hadn't stopped it in time. Did I look as vulnerable when he caught me watching him? He blinked away whatever I thought I'd seen.

Luke cleared his throat a few times. It squeezed my heart to think that the awkwardness between us had returned. You would think that our discussions of bed-wetting and motion sickness would have put an end to all that.

Still, I waited. He had to have something on his mind, and I wanted to give him the chance to say it before Sam came racing back. I had a little something to tell him, too.

"These past few weeks have been great," he said finally.

"Why do I feel a big old *but* coming on?"

He looked surprised that I'd asked it, but he gripped the round metal bar in front of him tighter. "No *but*. I've really had a nice time. I hate to admit it and I'll deny it if you ever tell her, but I'm glad my mom coerced me into coming to that anniversary party."

What would he think if he knew I wanted to kiss his mother for making him come that day almost as much as I wanted to kiss him again? The truth was he hadn't kissed me again since those sweet moments on the boat, and I was long overdue.

"But?" I prompted again.

He shook his head, frowning. "*But* I've enjoyed our time together, and I wish it didn't have to end."

"That's great because it doesn't have to. Not yet."

Luke looked perplexed with a little deer-caught-in-the-headlights thrown in for good measure. I tried to ignore the deer part, concentrating on clearing his confusion instead.

"Uncle Jack and Aunt Eleanor called this afternoon from Paris. They've decided to extend their vacation for two weeks. I've agreed to stay, too, to take care of Princess. I'll be here until at least Sunday the ninth."

Okay, I hadn't really expected cartwheels. Luke had never struck me as the cartwheel type. But I'd be lying if I said I didn't expect a little more than the "oh" that came out of his mouth then. Sure, he covered it with a less-than-enthusiastic "that's great," but the "oh" hung between us and sank like a helium balloon filled with peanuts instead.

"Sunday the ninth, huh? That's great."

I just wished he'd stop repeating it if he wasn't going to force a little enthusiasm into his voice. This wasn't making me feel all warm and fuzzy inside. Cold and scratchy, maybe, but definitely not warm and fuzzy.

Eighteen days and holding...but why?

His hands gripped the rail again, and he looked as if he might say something else, but Sam saved him from another platitude by racing out the ride's exit.

"That was cool. Can I ride it again?"

Luke smiled the smile he couldn't spare for me over my so-called good news. "Why don't you ride all of them first and then come back to the ones you've already ridden?"

Sam appeared to consider the logic in that before agreeing to the idea. "I want to ride the boats next."

I had to agree with his choice. I wanted to go back to my aunt and uncle's boat again, too.

Everything had seemed so clear while Luke and I were under that so-blue sky and floating among the gentle waves. How strange that it would be on dry land that I felt trapped in muddled waters.

"Lead the way," Luke told him.

We followed close behind him, and I was surprised when Luke took my hand again. The temptation to yank it free and hurry for the car was strong, but I couldn't do it. Even protecting my heart didn't seem a strong enough motivation. What could I say? I was a glutton for pain.

As Sam climbed to the front seat on one of the six tiny boats that floated in a doughnut-shaped metal tub, Luke leaned close to my ear.

"I'm really glad you're staying longer," he whispered.

I tried to ignore how good his breath felt feathering across my cheek and how desperately I wanted to believe what he was saying. I had to be earning my gold medal in the Pitiful Female Olympics.

Still, I had some dignity. "Well, you didn't sound like you were."

"You took me by surprise is all."

"Remind me never to give you a surprise party. You wouldn't make an attractive surprisee."

"I guess not."

I'd done it again, making reference to a future we both knew didn't exist, but he let it pass without comment.

The clamor from Sam and several other preschoolers ringing the bells next to their individual steering wheels made it impossible for us to hear even if we had more to say. We didn't. Luke just kept holding my hand, sometimes brushing his callused thumb over the back of my hand, and I kept letting him.

Before long we were back to our regular selves, talking and laughing together and watching Sam go round and round by motorcycle and race car and boat. I became determined to take it all in, to sip every taste of the day and breathe in every scent. I was determined to enjoy every bit of the now. There was a good chance that now was all we had.

Chapter Eleven

When I heard the car door outside the house that Monday night nearly two weeks later, I jumped up from the couch and glanced at the clock. It read 8:23 p.m. What happened to *five o'clock sharp?* So much for reservations for three at Gino's Taste of Italy.

So much for my big date on this all-important third of July.

Still, for a reason I couldn't understand let alone defend, I patted my hair that I'd fussed with earlier and smoothed my hands down my powder-blue floral sundress. If I still cared what Luke thought about my appearance when he hadn't bothered to show up before I started to wilt, I had more serious problems than being nearly stood up for a date.

I crossed the room, not even bothering to turn off the big-screen television, where Warren Beatty played opposite Natalie Wood in *Splendor in the Grass.* Too bad real-life romance couldn't be more like the old Hollywood version.

Was I allowed to be angry here? How soon into a new relationship was one of the partners allowed to make demands? Was the first month too soon? But then wasn't the first month also too soon to be taking a person for granted?

Ever since I'd announced that I would be extending my stay, Luke had been pulling away from me. Not a clear break like a "Dear John" letter, Luke's defection had been far subtler. He still called every day to make plans with Sam and me, but he just took his sweet time showing up for them. Each day it was a little later, until tonight he might as well not have shown up at all.

I stepped back into my black heels and crossed to the front door. The bell rang just as I reached it. Keeping my expression blank, I pulled open the door. Instead of the very late Luke Sheridan who I expected to be standing there, Yvonne stood on the stoop, holding Sam's hand.

"Hi, Miss Cassie."

No matter how frustrated I was, I couldn't help smiling down at the sweet little boy. "Hi, Sam. What are you doing with your grandma?"

"Grammy came to pick you up."

I turned to Yvonne, lifting an eyebrow. "Oh she did, did she?"

Yvonne pressed her lips together, her gaze darting from one side of the room to the other. "Luke had to work late again. He wanted me to bring you to the restaurant so he could meet you there. Sammy's already eaten."

"I see." I couldn't keep the disappointment out of my

voice. I wanted to believe it wasn't for myself but for the child who was once again spending too much time without his daddy, but I was feeling selfish. Besides the boy who was supposed to be suffering from this separation appeared as happy as a clam, while I was downright crabby.

"No, I don't think you do see," Yvonne said simply. "Do you mind if we come in for a minute?"

I shrugged and let them pass before closing the door behind them. By the time I reached the great room, Sam was already planted in front of the television. On the screen, a mentally fragile Deanie Loomis was raging against her young love, Bud Stamper, a hint to the bad ending ahead in the movie. Okay, sometimes art did imitate life. At least my life.

"Miss Cassie, can I put on cartoons?"

Sam already had the remote in his hand, but I took it from him and switched the channel myself.

"So you're into tearjerkers?" Yvonne indicated the TV screen that was now covered with little green Martians.

"Reflected my mood, I guess."

"Luke's really sorry he had to work late. He got called into a meeting with his boss."

I stepped over to the dinette and took one of the chairs, indicating for Yvonne to take the other.

"He said that when he called."

He'd also said he would be over just as soon as he could possibly get away, and I could see how well that had worked out for him. Now he was sending his mother over to do damage control with me, and I wasn't in the mood to be placated.

Even sitting still turned out to be impossible, so I popped up from my seat and went over to the coffeemaker to pour two cups. I'd been sipping caffeine since the first hour Luke was late, and now my insides sloshed and my hands trembled.

"Thank you." Yvonne accepted one of the heavy mugs between her hands.

"Cream or sugar?" I asked as an afterthought. If she asked for coffee cream, I wasn't even sure there was any in the house.

"Black. I prefer to keep things simple."

I was about to find out how simple, I had the feeling.

"I suppose Luke told you how important this job is to him, how Clyde Lewis put such trust in him," Yvonne said.

"He told me all of that, but I don't see how it makes a difference right now."

"Then you weren't listening."

I stared at her, trying not to be annoyed but failing. This was the second time she'd hinted that I was partially responsible for tonight's fiasco when blaming me was like holding the wet tennis shoes responsible for being left out in the rain. First, she'd told me I didn't see what was laid out in front of me, and now she was accusing me of not listening.

"Come on, Yvonne. I know it's hard for a parent not to take her child's side in an argument, but isn't this a little over-the-top?"

She only smiled, but then her expression grew serious again. "I loved my daughter-in-law. Don't ever question that. But I never thought she was good for my son."

I had just sipped my coffee, so I felt fortunate that I

didn't spew the brown liquid across the table. With effort, I managed to swallow it. Yvonne's revelation surprised me, but what did that have to do with Luke pulling away from me? "He told me about Nicole," I said, guessing she expected me to say something.

I'd surprised her, too. I could tell by the way she lifted her cup toward her mouth and then lowered it without taking a drink.

"He doesn't usually talk about her," she said finally.

"He said that, too."

Yvonne nodded and then pressed her hands on the edge of the table. "My son's been killing himself, trying to prove himself to someone who's no longer alive to appreciate his efforts. He's thrown himself into his work at the expense of everything else in his life."

"He said she always thought of him as a disappointment."

Settling back in her seat, Yvonne crossed her arms over her chest in a self-satisfied gesture. "Then you do understand."

Wait, had the two of us just participated in two parallel conversations? We must have. Otherwise, why would she guess that I understood something we hadn't even discussed as far as I could tell? "No, I don't think I do."

She frowned at me as if I was missing something incredibly simple. "In the last month since you've been here, I've seen more of my son in daylight hours than I have since his wife died. You reminded him to take the time to enjoy his son. To smell the roses, so to speak. To live his life."

I shook my head, as much to dispel her assumptions

as to deny the truth in them. "He didn't do those things for me. But it doesn't matter why he did it now because he's back to his workaholic ways, anyway. He comes later and later every day."

"Only because his boss demanded that he be there if he planned to keep his job."

I had been ready with a retort, but it died on my lips. I would have called it an "aha moment" if "duh" didn't seem to define it better. Luke had based his self-esteem on this job; of course he would panic if that job were in jeopardy. Would he ever learn not to judge himself based on everyone else's expectations?

"Do you see the problem now?" she asked.

I could only nod. That I did see didn't change anything, but I chose not to tell her that.

"Can you give him a break just this one time? I know how much he looked forward to tonight. Just let me take you to the restaurant. You two can have a nice quiet dinner and maybe talk a little."

"Why does this matter so much to you?"

"Because you're good for my son," Yvonne said. "It's been a long time since he's been around someone who's good for him, and I don't want him to mess this up."

Because she'd made a good mother's argument and because, let's face it, I'm a pushover, I agreed to go. I hadn't eaten dinner, either. And, if I gave myself some time, I would come up with a dozen or so other reasons why this was a perfectly rational decision. Maybe the biggest reason was that I enjoyed feeling as if I'd been run over by a pickup because I was well on my way to experiencing the first tire tracks.

* * *

Dinner couldn't have been more uncomfortable if Luke and I had sat cross-legged on a bed of nails, eating linguini. Even the checkered tablecloths, the globed candles and soft music failed to wrap us in a romantic cocoon.

Though I had a little in common tonight with Molly Ringwald's character in *Sixteen Candles,* Sam's sweet, tabletop birthday cake scene this was not.

"How's the lasagna?" Luke asked to break the silence. His own fork kept twisting in his plate of spaghetti and meatballs, but he hadn't taken a bite.

"Fine." Nothing against Gino's lasagna—it was probably scrumptious—but I might as well have been gnawing on cardboard for all I tasted it. "How's yours?"

He took a bite, chewed and swallowed so he could offer an opinion. "It's good." He spun his fork in the spaghetti for a long time before he spoke again. "I'm sorry about being late. It couldn't be helped."

"Your mom told me."

"I'm glad you agreed to come even though it was so late. I really wanted to see you tonight."

Really? If that was so, then why had he spent the whole time since he'd met me at Gino's acting as if he preferred to be right back at the building site he'd left an hour ago? He was so nervous, distracted. You could take a workaholic out of the office, but you couldn't take the office out of his head.

If I knew I was going to be this lonely at dinner, I would have stayed at home with *Splendor*'s Deanie and Bud. Even if they didn't end up together and she did have a nervous breakdown, at least they could argue passionately instead of being so annoying civil—the way we were.

"Really, I'm sorry."

I chewed and swallowed another bite. "It's fine."

"Is it?"

No, I wanted to shout. It wasn't okay for him to forget it was my birthday, as he so obviously had. When I looked up from my plate, Luke was studying me, his eyes narrowed.

"It's the new habit, anyway," I said.

"I should have explained before."

"Explained what? That you didn't want to see me anymore?"

I stabbed my fork into my lasagna.

He was shaking his head, but I was on a roll and couldn't stop.

"Ever since I told you I was staying on, you've been—I don't know—distant."

"Not distant. Just busy."

"Aren't they the same?"

"No, they're not." He shook his head to emphasize the point. "That would imply that I had a choice here, and I don't. Clyde has been breathing down my neck about cutting out of work early ever since you came here. I told him I would make it up after…"

Though he let his words trail off, I understood that he'd meant after I went home.

"So I messed up your plans by staying too long and wearing out my welcome?"

"No."

He started to reach for my hand across the table, but I went for my napkin and wiped my mouth instead. For a few seconds, he rested both hands on the table, palms up and fingers partially curled in, but then he returned them to his lap.

"I don't see it that way at all," he told me.

"Then how do you see it?"

I crossed my arms and waited for his answer. The waiter started toward us, but when he saw my tense pose, he wisely turned away, giving us a few extra minutes to decide whether our dinners were satisfactory.

"I'm glad you're still here. I want you here. But there was only so long I could let my work slide. Believe me, Clyde noticed it was sliding, too.

"I had to buckle down and make up for all the hours I was cutting, and when you said you were staying another week, I realized I couldn't wait any longer."

"What do you mean 'make up' for them?" But even as I asked it, realization dawned. "You mean you taking the time to put your family first—that was all just an act." Was the time he'd spent with me an act, as well?

"It wasn't like that, and you know it." At the edge of the table, his hands clenched and unclenched, showing his frustration.

I shook my head. Obviously, I didn't know Luke at all.

"Don't you get it? I'm doing the best I can."

"I don't know what I think, Luke."

"But I know."

I looked up at him. Was it hurt that I saw in his eyes? "You told me I was a good dad. I liked it that you thought so. I didn't want to lower your opinion of me, but I couldn't lose my job just to preserve that opinion."

"I never asked you to do anything."

He lifted an eyebrow. "Didn't you? Your approval comes with a price, and that's doing things your way."

"That's not fair, and you know it."

"Maybe not, but it's true."

I would have protested again if the waiter hadn't tried a second time, approaching the table and glancing nervously at our barely touched dinners. After assurances that the food was wonderful and hints that we couldn't take our lack of appetites out on his tip, he retreated to the kitchen.

Needless to say, our dinner date went downhill from there, and I'd thought we'd already reached the southernmost point of lousy. Only I would end up on a crummy date that was determined to be all it could be. Luke wouldn't even look at me, but I wasn't looking back, either. He'd hurt me, and I'd hurt him back. We were even, so why did it feel like we'd both lost?

The waiter didn't even bother to ask us if we wanted any spumoni. He just brought the check, processed Luke's credit card and packed both our dinners into to-go bags.

So much for the day I had dreaded for years and then looked forward to for the last few weeks. I'd imagined balloons and maybe a cake. None of my fantasies had included a dinner I couldn't eat and a dressing-down I didn't deserve.

As we stood to leave the restaurant, I leaned over and blew out the globed candle on the table. It was the only candle I would be blowing out tonight.

* * *

When I used to have problems at night, Mom would tell me to sleep on them. "Everything will be clearer in the morning," she would say.

But as I sat in the middle of my bed the next morning, my blankets tangled around me from an all-night wrestling match, I decided that clear had to be overrated since I wasn't any closer to seeing it. Maybe it was just better if we saw our mistakes through a foggy film than through sparkling glass.

First light filtered in through my partially open blinds. Sunshine and blue skies were in the forecast for today's Fourth of July celebrations, but it wasn't as if I had any place to go.

I expected to see Princess in the doorway, ready to start meowing for her breakfast, but I was alone. Just how early was it? The bedside clock said six forty-five. The least I could do on my vacation was to sleep in until eight.

Still, since I wouldn't be getting any more sleep this morning, I threw back the covers and climbed out of bed. I was still smoothing out the sheets when the doorbell rang. Could this morning get any stranger?

I slipped a summer-weight robe over my pajamas, and then hurried down the steps. At the front door, I patted my hair down and then hesitated. Serial killers didn't usually show up before seven o'clock, did they? And if they did, would they bother to ring doorbells to announce themselves?

"The early bird gets the worm," I whispered, the side of my mouth lifting as I thought of myself wiggling as the worm.

Pausing for one last yawn, I pulled open the door.

"Happy Fourth of July, Miss Cassie." Sam stood there holding a big bouquet of balloons, but they were pink and purple rather than the holiday's traditional red, white and blue.

Instead of waiting for an invitation that I was in no way ready to give, the little boy pushed past me into the house, first pummeling me with the balloons and then pulling them like a parachute after him.

Slowly, I turned back to the doorway, my heart pounding in my chest. I wasn't ready to see Luke again so soon, but I couldn't leave him out there on the porch either.

Luke stood in front of me with a white bakery box in his arms. He lowered his gaze to the box, and when he looked up again, he smiled.

"Happy birthday, Cassie."

I had no time to be shocked or happy or any of the other feelings that were mingling inside of me, each vying for a leadership role, because Luke leaned in and touched his lips to mine.

And I was lost. No matter how unclear my thoughts were when it came to last night and to the series of events leading up to it, my thoughts about Luke were filled with pinpoint precision. I was in love with him. So different from the way I'd felt about my former husband—admiring certain things about him—I loved Luke, all of him. I loved his strengths, I loved his flaws, and the truth in that unnerved me.

Being that vulnerable to another human being

seemed downright suicidal. Could I handle the pain when I lost him?

Luke pulled back slightly and pressed the box into my hands. I lifted the lid to find a birthday cake with pink roses all over it. A birthday greeting and my name were written in lavender script across the top.

"Sorry it's late."

"Don't you mean early?" I indicated with my hand toward the sun that was still low in the eastern sky.

He shrugged, grinning. "It's never too early to make things right, right?"

Because he posed it as a question and looked about as sheepish as a guy could, I smiled back. "Thank you. That was sweet." We couldn't continue standing there on the porch, especially me in my nighttime getup, so I stepped back to let him inside.

"I wanted to apologize about last night," he told me. "The things I said."

"You've already apologized."

"Last night I didn't even know everything I'd done wrong. Now I do." He shook his head. "No wonder you were so mad at me. I can't believe I forgot your birthday. It's just with everything going on— No. There's no excuse."

"I could have reminded you." I could also tell him that he'd missed the point for at least part of my frustration with him, but I still hadn't worked out in my mind if I'd had any right to those feelings.

"You shouldn't have had to."

"Why aren't you at work?" I glanced away as I asked the loaded question. What was I fishing for, a fight?

"Haven't you heard, it's Independence Day? Even poor schmucks like me get the day off today. Besides, I couldn't talk a single subcontractor into working today." He shot a glance past me. "We'd better go see what's he's up to."

I led him deeper into the house and set the cake on the kitchen counter. Sam was running around the family room in a circle, the balloons trailing behind him. Princess yawned in the recliner, looking unimpressed by the performance.

"Hey Sam, those balloons are for Miss Cassie, remember?" Luke called out to him.

Sam slowed long enough to yell "Happy birthday" and kept right on running.

"Oh, let him have fun for a few minutes. I'll have to get dressed before I run around the family room with my balloons, anyway."

Luke grinned at my attempt at humor and crossed back to the counter. Lifting the lid off the box again, he glanced down at the cake. "I didn't figure you'd want it to say 'thirty' on it or anything."

"Thirty's not so bad. Better than the alternative."

"Three decades looks great on you."

I couldn't help chuckling at that. "You could have picked a better time to say that to me." Reflexively, I patted my hair again, wondering just how much of it was sticking out in all directions.

He reached up and brushed back my hair himself. "You couldn't look bad if you tried. Not to me."

"Sounds like a challenge."

"Hmm, maybe I shouldn't have suggested that. I know what an overachiever you can be."

I smiled. We were back to our easy banter, but it felt forced today. Just as I started to excuse myself to my room to change, Sam came roaring toward us, a trail of colors behind him.

"Did you tell her, Daddy?"

"You mean ask her. No, I didn't ask her yet."

I looked back and forth between them, before crouching in front of Sam. "What did you want to ask me?"

"There's a bicycle parade."

"Parade?" I turned to Luke for clarification.

"We thought it would be fun if the three of us went to the Mantua Fourth of July Parade. It's about the biggest thing around here until Santa shows up in the Christmas parade. You'll have to wait until November for that."

I tried to ignore his last comment and the squeezing feeling it produced inside my heart. November was a long time away, and I'd never be around to greet old Saint Nick.

"It begins this early?"

"No. Ten o'clock."

Ten o'clock? Above the stove, I glanced at the microwave clock. Because the numbers read only 6:57, I turned back to him and raised an eyebrow.

"We need to get there ahead of time," Luke explained.

"Tough to get a seat on the parade route?"

"We won't be sitting."

"We're riding bikes in the parade." Sam was springing up and down as he made his announcement.

I shook my head. It was way too early in the morning for any of this. I needed to crawl back into bed and pull the sheet over my head. Maybe when I awoke again, everything would be back to normal, if there was such a thing. "No, I don't think—"

"Come on. It'll be an adventure."

Adventure? It sounded like holiday torture to me.

Luke continued as if I was already on board. "Sam and I did this last year. This time he gets to ride his own bike."

"With training wheels," Sam chimed in.

"I don't even have a bike." I would have said I'd left mine at home, but I didn't have one there, either. By choice.

"I borrowed my mom's this morning." Luke told me. "All we have to do is decorate it."

"Great."

That my response wasn't exactly infused with enthusiasm only made Luke laugh.

"I haven't ridden a bike in over ten years, Luke."

"You knew how to ride one before that, right?" He waited for my nod before he continued. "Then you haven't forgotten how. Come on. You'll have fun."

"Yeah, Miss Cassie, please. We have streamers and balloons and everything." Sam's eyes shone as he described it, and he looked so hopeful. It was going to be hard saying no to a face like that.

"Not those balloons," Luke corrected, pointing at the bundle dancing above his son's head. "Those are for Miss Cassie's birthday."

"It was yesterday," Sam pointed out needlessly.

Luke frowned at his son. "Don't keep reminding me."

"You forgot."

"Yeah."

The sadness on Luke's face as he glanced back at me brought me to a decision. "Okay, let's go be in a parade." A thought crossed my mind then. "Did you say you picked up the bike from your mom earlier *this morning?* I hope you gave her a big present on Mother's Day."

"I didn't wake her. I just used my key to the garage."

"Lucky her."

His gaze narrowed. "You weren't in bed, were you?"

I shook my head.

His grin returned. "You see then, it's all good."

"Yeah, it's all good."

Luke rounded the counter and came up behind me, propelling me toward the stairs. "Now that that's settled, why don't you go get ready? By the time you get back, Sam and I will have breakfast à la Sheridan waiting. We'll make sure Princess gets her breakfast, too."

"You don't have to do all that."

"We do if we're going to get you out of this house before the parade goes rolling through downtown." He pointed to the stairs. "Now hurry."

I followed his instructions and returned to my room, showering and putting on a holiday-appropriate red T-shirt and navy shorts. This wasn't the outing I would have planned, but it still was time with Luke and Sam. Each hour was becoming more precious, and each minute felt like sand through the hourglass with nothing to stop the spray.

How was I going to leave here on Sunday? I had to; I knew that. I had a whole life back in Toledo and students that needed me. But I didn't have to kid myself: a part of me would stay behind in Mantua.

Chapter Twelve

The parade was a tiny but festive event, with plenty of flag waving and fanfare. Firefighters in their full uniforms tossed out candy from their shiny yellow trucks and flipped their sirens on and off for the crowd. A senior women's choir belted out patriotic selections. The county fair queen and her court waved from their perches atop the backs of convertibles.

In the middle of all that, eighty-some bicycles, tricycles and bike trailers rolled along in full regalia down the four square blocks that constituted downtown and to the neighborhoods beyond. We couldn't compete with the rose-covered floats in the Rose Parade, and our balloons didn't have the impact of the flying creatures in Macy's Thanksgiving Day Parade, but our event had its own charm.

In fact, the whole thing was such a slice of Americana that I half expected somebody to show up with a sack full of baseballs, someone else with hot dogs and a third person with a steaming apple pie.

At Sam's insistence, Luke, Sam and I were right near the front, breathing diesel fumes from the fire engine and gripping the handlebars with one hand while waving to our fans with the other. Our bikes were works of art, masterpieces of balloons, streamers and rolls of colored tape. We'd even attached streamers to our helmets to complete the effect.

To my credit, I managed to keep the bike upright and didn't once run into that back bumper of the fire engine. I could guess who would end up on the losing end of that collision. Luke was right, anyway: I hadn't forgotten my bicycle riding skills.

Though I would pay for today's outing tomorrow, with all the pain decidedly *behind* me, I enjoyed the burn in my muscles and the exhilaration in my chest.

Marcus and Yvonne were waiting for us when we reached the end of the parade route at the entrance to Lakeside Park.

"You look great on my bike," Yvonne told me.

She was just being kind. If anything, I looked exhausted and windburned, but I thanked her anyway.

"Feel free to use it any time you like. I'm not clocking enough miles on the bike, and the old girl could probably use the exercise."

I nodded, though I wouldn't get the chance to ride again before I left, and we both knew it.

"That's right, Mom. She could use some exercise." Luke grinned at the dirty look his mother gave him over his referring to a different *she.*

"Well, I know someone who isn't getting any lunch today. Are the rest of you ready for the picnic?"

Yvonne held out the picnic basket she had draped over her arm.

"Picnic?" I asked blankly, noticing for the first time that everyone around us had similar baskets and were carrying blankets and coolers like those Marcus had at his feet.

Luke climbed off his bike and flipped down the kick-stand. "Oh, we didn't tell you about that? The parade ends at the park, where the whole town meets for a picnic."

I turned back to him. "You didn't mention any of that earlier. Why not?"

"You were half-asleep when we came over. I didn't want to overload your mind with too much information at once."

Yvonne looked at me with that warm, welcoming smile I was coming to know well. "We're hoping you'll join us, Cassie. We have plenty."

I had the sense that these arrangements had been made long before Luke and Sam had shown up at the beach house that morning, but I decided to be a good sport. "I hate to come empty-handed. The least I could have done was bring my birthday cake."

The side of Yvonne's mouth lifted. "Where exactly would you have carried it?"

I glanced where I was standing on the ground and straddling the bar of the bicycle. She had a point.

"It's the thought that counts, Cassie." Luke reached over to squeeze my shoulder. "Now let's go eat. I'm starving."

"Me, too, Daddy."

Sam rolled ahead on his bike, straight into the crowd entering through the park's black-iron gate. Marcus grabbed his load and hobbled after Sam, preventing a catastrophe at least for the moment. With Luke and I walking our bikes and Yvonne carrying the basket, we eventually reached Sam and his grandfather and continued with them toward a spot that Sam chose, not far from the edge of a narrow stream. We parked our three bikes a few feet from the picnic site.

"How long do you think it will be before this one ends up in the water?" Marcus indicated with his head toward his grandson as we spread the heavy quilt on the ground.

"Better not happen at all." Luke turned a warning look on his son. "I don't have another set of clothes with me."

"You? Unprepared?" Marcus looked incredulous as he set his cooler next to one of the park's grills and pulled a small bag of charcoal briquettes, grilling supplies, a package of hot dogs and some tinfoil from the cooler.

"I've had other things on my mind."

His job, I figured. What else?

Marcus nodded and winked. It seemed like a strange reaction to me. Didn't he care how many hours Luke had left Sam in their care lately? If it didn't bother them, it was never going to become an issue for Luke.

Yvonne set the basket on the blanket and started pulling small plastic containers from the basket. After the first five, I began to wonder if she was performing an illusion, setting a basket with a trap door above a stocked refrigerator or something.

She looked embarrassed when she caught me watching. "Just a little of everything."

Yvonne was right. She did have everything in there: coleslaw, veggies, deviled eggs, potato salad, five-cup salad and a bag of slightly smashed hot dog buns, plus condiments, plates and napkins.

I helped her put serving spoons in all the dishes, covering them with their lids to keep bugs out of them. "Everything looks great," I told her.

"You outdid yourself, as always, Mom," Luke called from where he and his father were standing by the grill.

If Yvonne pulled out an apple pie next I was going to pass out right there on the spot. Already around us it looked like a Norman Rockwell summer scene—all about families and warmth and caring.

This was a real community, where people brought casseroles to sick neighbors, met for coffee and remembered birthdays. I might have found that kind of community in Toledo, as well, but I'd never slowed down enough to realize I wanted it. And I did want it, so much it hurt.

As I scanned the crowd, my gaze landed on Luke, who was laughing with his father. He had none of the strain I'd seen around his eyes lately, and his mouth had lost its hard line. He caught me watching him and winked at me before turning away to pour lighter fluid over the charcoal so Marcus could light the fire. Sam was nearby, crouched down on the ground and poking something with a stick.

Yes, I longed for community, but I longed for family even more. This family. This man and this child. The idea of driving away from them was tearing me apart.

"I forgot to tell you happy birthday."

Quickly turning back toward the voice, I found Yvonne watching me. Her smile was a knowing one.

"Oh, thanks."

"Luke told me he feels lousy for forgetting," she said in a low voice. "You make sure he keeps feeling lousy for a while. You'll be able to hold that over his head for a long time."

I shrugged and started messing with the plates for something to do with my hands. "It was no big deal." I kept my voice low. I didn't have a long time to hold his forgetting my birthday over his head, anyway, not with only five days until I packed up for home.

Five days and holding.

"No big deal? I would hang Marcus up by his toenails if he forgot my birthday, and he knows it. I'd also make sure he didn't forget his mistake anytime soon."

"I thought we learned in church to forgive each other?" I gave her my best censuring frown, but it quickly transformed into a smile. I had seen the way Marcus and Yvonne looked at each other, much the same as Uncle Jack and Aunt Eleanor did, even after all of these years. Marcus was probably safe, even if he did mess up a time or two.

"We wives forgive, but it's a long time before we forget. Marcus says wives have memories like elephants, whatever that means."

"I'm not sure." But maybe Marcus was on to something, even if he was comparing women to humongous animals without good table manners or fashion sense. I'd been a wife, and I still hadn't forgotten. I'd like to say I'd forgiven, but the jury was still out on that, too.

"What are you two beautiful ladies whispering about over here?" Marcus asked as he carried a plate of hot dogs over to us. "Do you need me to flex so you can get a better look at the old physique?"

Yvonne laughed out loud at that. "No, we're fine. We wouldn't want you to strain yourself or anything."

He made a mean face at his wife and then dropped a kiss on her head.

"Hey, Sam, lunch is ready," Luke called out. "Come over here and eat."

The boy looked up from his newest demolition project, this time an ant hill, a stick his instrument of doom. He popped up and scampered back, leaving the ants to repair the destruction.

Once we were all seated, Marcus reached out his hands, and we all joined in a circle.

"Father, thank You for this fine holiday and the blessing of all this food. Thank You for our friends and neighbors, who share this time and space with us. And a special thanks, Lord, for sending Cassie our way. In the name of Christ our Lord. Amen."

Luke squeezed my hand before he let it go. "Boy, I thought the food was going to get cold before you got around to finishing that one, Dad."

"You really know how to hurt a guy," Marcus said, but he was laughing.

I wondered if Luke's joke was for my benefit. His father had thanked God for sending me to them. It seemed like such a strange prayer of thanksgiving when I was on borrowed time here.

We made quick work of all the food, sharing stories

and laughter along with the potato salad. When we were clearing away the empty containers, Yvonne produced yet another box from her basket of surprises. Chocolate chip cookies and peanut butter cookies were stacked inside.

"Now you're just spoiling me," I said, taking one of each.

"We're doing our best." Luke reached over and laid his hand across the one I was resting on the blanket. "Me, especially."

My breath hitched, which wouldn't have been such a big deal if I hadn't just taken a big bite of the chocolate chip cookie. The sweet treat took a wrong turn, straight down my windpipe. I started an immediate round of spasmodic coughing into my napkin. No matter how hard I tried, I couldn't stop.

"She's choking. Smack her on the back," Marcus called out.

"No, don't do that," Yvonne insisted. "If she's coughing, she's still getting oxygen."

"Son, do you know the Heimlich?" Marcus piped again.

"It's not necessary." Instead, Luke reached over and rubbed my back for support more than assistance.

By the time I caught my breath again, tears trailed down my cheeks.

"Are you okay, sweetheart?" Yvonne asked.

Seeing her concern, I nodded.

Luke brushed my tears away with his thumb. "I was hoping to change your life. I wasn't expecting to have to save it."

The others laughed at Luke's comment—even Sam

who thought it was the best thing since a knock-knock joke—but I couldn't join in. Change my life? What was he saying?

Luke turned back to me and took both of my hands in his. Strange, until now we'd been in the middle of a crowd of enthusiastic picnickers. At this moment we weren't even alone on this quilt that Marcus, Yvonne and Sam shared. Yet, somehow as I sat staring into those startling blue eyes, there didn't seem to be anyone else in the park—in the world—besides the two of us.

"Cassie, I know we haven't known each other for very long—"

"Only most of our lives," I added before I could stop myself.

Luke gave me a tense grin. "You know what I mean. Anyway, what I was trying to say was that I—"

"Oh!"

We both turned toward the sound of the interruption. Luke and I weren't alone after all, and his dad sat across from us, wearing a grimace. "Sorry, I forgot the... thing...in the cooler."

Marcus crouched next to it and opened the lid, withdrawing a sealed plastic container from beneath the ice. I put up my hand to stop another onslaught of food. Why was everyone force-feeding me? Didn't they realize I was already back to my fighting weight? If they didn't stop soon, I was going to be as plump as the Thanksgiving turkey, four months early and without the corn bread stuffing.

Instead of me, though, Marcus handed the container to his son, who thanked him for it and set it next to him. Before pulling open the lid, Luke glanced across the blanket to the others, who apparently had been there all along.

"Does anyone else have a comment to make, or are you going to let me finish?"

Yvonne shook her head as she stuffed another cookie in Sam's mouth so he didn't get the chance, either. "No, you go right ahead."

I was thinking the same thing. In fact, I would have told him to spit it out already if I thought it would get the answers to me any sooner.

Luke turned back to me and tilted his head to the side. "Third time's a charm. As I was saying—" he paused to frown at the list of candidates who might interrupt yet again "—I love you, Cassie."

I blinked. My gaze lowered to my clenched hands. Had I heard him right? I'd imagined him saying it out loud someday and talked myself out of believing it was possible, but here it was, and I couldn't find the words to answer him.

When I glanced up at him, Luke studied me cautiously as he gripped the container in his hands. "Now would be the time to say something. Uh…if you want."

Snapped out of my daze, I shook my head to clear it. Could he actually believe I didn't— No. How could he ever think such a thing when I wanted to be with him more than anything I'd ever wanted?

"Well then, this has been fun, but…" As he spoke, he started collecting remaining plates and utensils into a garbage bag, backing away from me at the same time.

"You're not getting off that easily."

He stopped with one plastic fork still suspended on its way to the trash. One eyebrow raised, he waited.

"I love you, too." I managed to say it in an even voice though I considered shouting it. I might as well have, as much of Mantua's citizenry was watching us. Everyone around us appeared to be in on the joke, and I'd yet to hear the punch line. The temptation to search for a hidden camera created a tickle up my spine.

"Well, that's good to hear." He spoke in a quiet, conspiratorial voice, for my ears alone. "I was afraid I was in this love business all by myself."

Then in front of God and everybody, he leaned in and kissed me full on the mouth. I used to think I had a problem with public displays of affection, but as he touched his lips to mine again, I wondered if it had been my issue at all. I didn't care who saw me here necking in public with the man I loved.

"I have something for you," he said as he pulled away and settled back on his haunches.

He reached for the container he'd put aside and pulled off its lid. Inside was a huge sugar cookie with pink frosting and purple sprinkles and my name in white script across the top. The whole thing was a perfect complement to the balloons I had back at the house.

"Happy birthday, Cassie!"

Even if his grin hadn't had a bit of sneakiness to it, I still would have been on guard. "Now I know this is a conspiracy. You're just trying to make me eat until I explode. This and the cake?"

He rolled his eyes at my silliness. "You at least want to try it, don't you?"

I shook my head and puffed up my cheeks. "Not just yet. I couldn't eat another bite right now, but thank you. It was so sweet of you to have it made for me. I'll try it later, after some of this big meal wears off."

Already I was wondering how I'd be able to get back on that bike and ride to my aunt and uncle's after eating so much.

"You wouldn't want me to think you don't appreciate my gift, would you?"

Of course I wouldn't, but why would he? I'd said thank you and everything. What did he expect, a back flip? If riding a bike was an iffy activity for me right now, then gymnastics was out of the question. When I frowned at him, he only smiled.

"Come on, just one bite."

"Fine."

My voice sounded harsher than I'd intended, and my exasperated breath was strong enough to rustle nearby trees. Still, I reached over to take the container from him. Eating with an audience would probably prove challenging, and I wasn't kidding when I said I couldn't eat any more, but I was going to sink my teeth into that pink frosting, chew and even swallow if it killed me.

Lifting out the cookie, I raised it to my mouth for a big bite. Just as the confection touched my lips and the smell of the rich frosting invaded my senses, the sunlight glinted off my cookie. I'd eaten plenty of cookies in my day, but I couldn't remember any before that could salve my sweet tooth *and* refract light.

The early morning and lack of sleep the night before

were probably just taking their toll, but I took a closer look at my name written in decorator icing, anyway. There in the dot above the *i* was a beautiful—and very messy—diamond ring. I couldn't do anything but stare, my limbs numb and my jaw falling open.

"So, do you like my cookie?" he asked, grinning. He reached over and plucked the ring from its goopy circle of icing, wiping the icing off the best he could with a napkin.

"I don't understand."

"It seems self-explanatory to me."

Maybe it should have been, but it wasn't. Thoughts of rings and vows swirled through my mind. That I thought absently of the choking hazard the ring had presented when I'd already survived one near-Heimlich experience this afternoon gave me a clue that I wasn't on my game here.

"I know what you're thinking. I guess it is a two-for-one cheapskate gift to give you the ring for your birthday, but I promise to make it up next year."

Next year? There would be a next year for us? I could hardly wrap my mind around the thrill in that. "Let me state for the record that you are an especially lousy mind reader."

"Good. That'll keep me guessing."

"Daddy, are you asking Miss Cassie to marry you?" chimed the little voice of reason that I recognized.

Luke made one of those frustrated sounds in his throat. "I'm getting around to it. Give me a minute, will you?"

"Sorry," Yvonne whispered, trying to ply Sam with yet another cookie.

I was still focused on the boy who would probably have a tummy ache later and on murmured conversations around us that kept including the name "Luke" when I heard the man in question call my name.

"Cassie," he said when I faced him. He had repositioned in front of me so that he was down on one knee. All the humor was absent from his gaze, but there was warmth there that spoke more clearly to my heart than his words ever could.

"I know we haven't known each other for very long—not as grown-ups anyway—but I feel as though you've been here all of my life." He indicated with his hand the chest cavity, which cradled his heart.

My own heart squeezed, and I nodded. I felt it, too, as if Luke had always been there, always intended for me.

"I love you more than I thought I could ever love anyone," he said. "You're more than I wanted for myself, certainly more than I deserve."

I leaned forward, shaking my head. "No, Luke, you deserve every—"

He raised his hand to stop me. "Are you going to let me finish this or not?"

I gestured for him to go ahead, feeling tense and excited and slightly nauseated, all at the same time.

"Please marry me, Cassie. I think we can make a life together. A long, happy life."

It was too sudden. Too rash. We needed to think about this, not make life-changing decisions on the spur of the moment. We still had too many questions to answer before we leaped, too many details to handle about melding two very separate lives into one.

And yet the romantic in me battled the pragmatist. If we loved each other, all the other pieces would fall neatly into place. Wouldn't they?

Why was I questioning? I loved Luke and Sam and wanted nothing more than to build a family and a future with them. Like Aunt Eleanor had suggested, I needed to learn to trust.

"Yes, I'll marry you," I heard myself say, though the confidence with which I said it surprised even me. It was the right thing, and Luke was the right man for me.

With a smile, Luke swept toward me, enclosing me in the comforting circle of his arms. He pressed his lips to mine in a kiss of commitment. That I already knew Luke kept his commitments made the promise even sweeter. "I love you, Cassie," he breathed against my skin.

When he pulled back, he held the ring out in front of me. Nervously, I extended my hand, and he slipped it on my finger. I looked down at the simple, round solitaire, sitting primly on my finger, its frosting-clouded facets catching the light and causing the colors of the spectrum to dance.

I was to be married again. This time to Luke, who loved me. Not to me with potential, but me.

His hand grasping my fingers where the ring of his promise now rested, Luke drew me in for another kiss. Applause had us pulling apart faster than probably either of us would have preferred. We had an audience, all right. People all around us were staring our way, smiling and shouting their congratulations. Good news must travel fast in Mantua, I concluded, even faster with help.

"The ring bearer's marrying the flower girl," I heard someone tell the woman next to her.

I suppose we did have a quaintness about us that would be downright irresistible to the romantic set. Which other couples had that kind of history, that kind of tale to tell their grandchildren?

The rest of the afternoon was wonderful: blue skies, a light breeze to keep the bugs at bay and enough activity to make sure even active little boys stayed occupied.

All day, I kept catching Sam watching me, wide-eyed as if he was seeing me for the first time. Each time he crawled up in my lap, I felt the weight of the responsibility I had accepted with his father's ring. No matter how many times I would gently explain that I wouldn't try to replace his mother, the truth remained that I was the only mother Sam would ever know.

In the hours for lawn dart playing and merry-go-round spinning that would continue until the fireworks at dusk, Luke couldn't have been more attentive: touching my shoulder, smiling a secret smile and looking at me as if I was the most precious woman in the world.

He even let me in on the secret that he'd planned to propose the evening before at Gino's, and he'd been so preoccupied with those plans that he'd forgotten the other thing that had been significant about July third.

For a day so perfect, I couldn't understand the seed of doubt that planted itself inside my heart and refused to budge. I loved Luke, right? And I wanted to be his wife and stepmother to Sam, right? The answer to both was a vehement yes. So why did I get the sense that all wasn't perfect in this worldly paradise?

Chapter Thirteen

The Michigan sky rained for the next three days straight. Oh, it had probably tapered off now and then and even fully stopped for a few intervals in those seventy-two hours, but I never saw anything but the downpour. Outside the window and inside my heart.

I glanced down at my hand as I waited for the microwave to beep, announcing that my TV dinner was ready. Sure enough, the engagement ring was still on my fourth finger. That whole Fourth of July holiday hadn't been just a figment of my imagination if it had produced hardware.

There were other reminders, too—other proof that I hadn't just made the whole day up after too much sunshine and too much alone time along the coast. The muscles in my backside still smarted from the strain of the bicycle parade, even though I hadn't had to make any return journeys on two wheels after the fireworks. Luke and his dad had loaded all three bikes into the back of his truck.

The cake, minus the slices we'd eaten after the fireworks, still rested on the counter in its box, becoming staler by the minute. The balloons would have still been around, too, if they hadn't lost their helium punch and lay on the floor as a temptation for Princess. After catching her chewing on one of the ribbons, I'd punctured their latex skin and disposed of them and their strings before the silly girl hurt herself.

I sat at the table and pulled the plastic film off the chicken something-or-other and the souped-up green beans. I didn't know why I'd even made it because I would only pick at it the way I had the rest of my meals the last few days.

I hadn't been totally alone during this time, not if you counted the calls from Luke and from Aunt Eleanor. His calls had been to tell me he had to work late and to cancel plans each night. Hers to let me know how much she looked forward to seeing me—and the ring—and then to let me know about delays from Charles de Gaulle International Airport out of Paris. They wouldn't make it back until Saturday after all.

"It's just you and me again, Princess."

At the noise, the kitty looked up from her bowl, but hunger overcame her curiosity about me. One of us at least still had an appetite. It was too late at night to be eating anyway.

Two days and holding.

What was I holding out for anyway? If it was for more time with Luke, I was holding out in vain. He'd asked me to marry him, and though we had so many details to work out before I left the state, I hadn't seen his face in two days. His family probably hadn't seen it, either. If home was where the heart was, then Luke's true home must have been at the office.

He wouldn't have made the time to see me tonight if I hadn't begged. Demanded was more like it, but a gal had to do what a gal had to do. Now I listened for his truck outside. He'd promised he'd be over soon, but that was nearly an hour ago. Clearly, Luke and I had different definitions of "soon."

Misgivings that had whispered to me the other day weren't bothering to whisper anymore and were shouting now. Hadn't I already lived this life? No, that was ridiculous. Luke couldn't have been more different from my ex and still have been a member of the human species. Yet I remembered those lonely, empty hours at home. This wasn't my home and Luke and I weren't even married yet, and I was already feeling I'd walked this road once before.

I twisted the ring back and forth on my finger, watching the facets pick up the overhead light, moving and swaying along the ceiling. Strange how it didn't shine as brightly this time.

When I finally heard the truck in the drive, I steadied myself and strode with resignation to the door. Luke stood on the porch, his expression mirroring my dark thoughts, but still he stepped forward and gathered me into his arms. He placed a single kiss on my lips before stepping back.

"Oh man, have I missed you," he said as if he meant it.

My eyes burned, and something in my throat thickened. I had to look away from him to keep from embarrassing myself by crying.

"I'm glad you talked me into coming tonight," he continued.

"I've been here all week." I wouldn't do any good to point out that he could have seen me, or his family, if he'd made the time. For whatever reason, he hadn't.

"I know. I'm sorry."

Taking my hand, Luke led me to the kitchen table and sat in the seat next to mine. Under the lights, he looked bone weary with dark circles of exhaustion beneath his eyes. Though I recognized that he'd brought all of it on himself, I still longed to reach out and let him sleep on my shoulder.

"Things have just been crazy at work lately, but I promise it will be better soon for you and Sam and me, just as soon as—"

"It will always be something else, won't it?"

Luke had been about to tell me of some deadline or completion date after which our lives would be filled with sunshine and flowers, but he closed his mouth at my words. I'd heard promises like those before, and I refused to gullibly accept them now.

"We're back to this again?" he said finally. "My job? You have no idea what I'm dealing with right now."

"I guess I don't. Why don't you tell me then? Maybe I could help."

The strained look he gave me made me wonder if there really was more to his work situation than just repaying his boss for playing hooky on my account. Maybe it was something serious and even temporary. Then he shook his head, and all my magnanimous thoughts fled.

"It's nothing. Nothing I can't handle."

"Why don't you ask Sam how well you've handled it so far? Or how many times you've had dinner with him lately. That's not going to get better, you know."

His jaw flexed and then he appeared to compose himself before speaking again. "You agreed to marry me. I would have thought that the least I could expect was some support from you."

"I'm trying to do that. But don't you see? The more you give up of your life—time with Sam and with me—the more that boss of yours is going to expect you to sacrifice. Haven't you given enough?"

"What do *you* expect me to do, Cassie? Quit? How will I provide for you and Sam if I do that?"

"Provide for us?" I planted my hands on the table. "I never asked you to do that. I have a perfectly good career that I've worked very hard to build. With my income, we could more than decently get by, and you—"

At Luke's shocked expression, I stopped.

"But I assumed," he began, but let his words fall away.

"You never asked me." Resting my elbows on the table, I lowered my head into the cradle of my hands. "It sounds like you assumed a lot of things, like that I would automatically give up my entire life in Ohio to move here."

And that I would come here to raise Sam for his absentee father, but I didn't add that.

"Why wouldn't I assume that we'd live here? Sam's life is here. My family is here. *Your* family is here."

"The point is we haven't even talked about it yet. You know I'm leaving, and you couldn't even make it over here for the last two days so we can make such important decisions about our future as where we're going to live."

"I told you I have a lot to deal with at work right now. If you'd just give me a chance to figure it out—"

"Work is always going to come first for you, isn't it? You say that family is your priority, but that's just lip service. Sam and your parents and now even I are always going to be waiting for you to figure out what's more important."

I expected him to be angry. That was one of the usual reactions to tough love like I was giving him. What I didn't expect was the grim smile that appeared on his lips.

"It must be nice being you, Cassie. Not all of us have the luxury of sitting on our high horses and pushing our values on everyone else. Some of us are just muddling through, trying to get by."

My stomach clenched, and I could no longer stay seated. I paced to the family room, pausing by the slider to turn back to Luke. "This isn't about me, though it does affect me. It's about you reevaluating your priorities."

Luke came to his feet and stalked toward me. "Cassie, you knew who I was when you agreed to marry me. You know my commitments are important to me. All of them."

I started to interrupt him, to tell him that some commitments simply must rank higher than others, but he shook his head to stop me.

He crossed his arms over his chest. "You knew that I've been breaking my back to make something of myself, to prove myself to everyone, to make my son proud. You knew that was the man I am when you said you'd marry me."

"I shouldn't have said yes."

The words escaped before I could stop them, but once they were out there, hanging between us like an impenetrable fog, I realized I had spoken the truth.

Luke's head jerked as if I'd slapped him, and I felt as if I had. Raw pain on his face mirrored what I was feeling in my heart.

"I'm sorry, Luke. I love you, but I can't marry you." My voice sounded tired, resigned. "I can never marry another man who doesn't put his family before his career."

My eyes didn't even bother heating this time before the tears came, and I didn't bother trying to stop them.

Slipping the ring off my finger, I put it in my left palm and extended that hand to him. Already my finger felt bare of the weight and the promise. I loved Luke. Until this very minute I didn't know how much. But loving him didn't mean I could offer myself as a doormat for him to trample. His respect was as important to me as his love.

At first he looked down at the ring in my hand as if it was something loathsome. When I'd held my hand out for so long that it ached, he finally reached over and plucked the ring from my palm and pocketed it. I swiped at the tears streaming down my cheeks.

Luke regarded my tears but looked away before he spoke again. "Good thing we got that settled. I would hate to think you'd make an awful mistake by marrying someone like me."

He shrugged as if this conversation mattered no more to him than the weather forecast, though he couldn't hide the vein that ticked at his temple. "I guess the whole thing between us got out of hand for you, especially when you only started seeing me to get closer to my son."

"You know that's not true."

"Isn't it?" he asked with a smirk. "You never loved me for me…if you loved me at all."

I had to fist my hands at my sides because I wanted to reach out and shake some sense into him. "You're wrong. I know the real you, and that's the man I love." I saw the denial in his eyes. "You're the only one who can't accept you for the person you are. You're the only one who still thinks you have something to prove."

"You'd understand if you had kids." There was challenge in his eyes as he said it.

He was hurting, and he wanted me to hurt, but I wasn't going to let him push that sensitive button to get to me this time.

"You could be right. Maybe I would. But I do know Sam. I was almost his stepmother, remember?" I had to pause then because the pain of losing that child of my heart was second only to the loss of his father. "You don't have to do anything to make Sam proud of you. You're his daddy. That's enough."

"I want him to look up to me, but I don't expect you to understand that." He glanced past me out the window that faced the dark water. "You've had people looking up to you all your life."

"Do you want Sam to grow up being proud of your accomplishments but be a complete stranger to you?"

I waited for the weight of my words to sink in and for him to strike back, but I didn't expect it to hurt so much when he did.

"This coming from the person who's so willing to leave here and drop out of our lives forever? You don't get parting shots, Cassie. You don't want to be a part of our lives, a part of our family, so just mind your own business."

With that, he patted the pocket where he'd shoved the engagement ring, turned and strode to the door. He didn't slam it, but its quiet click reverberated in my ears. Nothing had ever felt so final. Doing the right thing had never felt like such a mistake.

My stomach growled for the third time in the last ten minutes, which shouldn't have come as any surprise. I could have eaten a bowl of Raisin Bran four hours ago when I'd started my mad cleaning frenzy, but I'd been too busy scrubbing toilets and adding my tears to the suds to take the time. My aunt and uncle would be here by early afternoon, and I wanted their home to be perfect.

Now I had only sparkling porcelain, shiny floors and burning eyes to show for my efforts, but I kept moving to stay ahead of my thoughts. Fat lot of good it had done me. I'd seen Luke's face in the shiny wood grain while I dusted, replayed our last conversation in the buzz of the dishwasher.

It was only right that a whirlwind romance would end in a whirlwind breakup. What would Aunt Eleanor say when I told her? Would she still tell me to trust and wait on God?

It was strange. This time I knew I was doing the right thing for the right reasons, but I wasn't prepared for how much it would hurt. We weren't even together very long, but I couldn't imagine a future without Luke in it. I'd pictured myself as Luke's wife and Sam's stepmother, and now I was having an awfully hard time blotting that image from my memory.

I sprayed the mirror in the great room with ammonia cleaner and started wiping with a paper towel. As the smeared glass cleared, I caught sight of my reflection and stared. My skin was blotchy, and my eyes were swollen and red.

My aunt and uncle probably expected that I would look better than when I had first arrived, and they should have been right. I was no longer as gaunt, and even with the sunscreen, I had earned some healthy-looking color. But if my relatives got a load of me right now, they would be sorry they'd ever left me to my own devices while they traveled across France.

Putting the cleaners back in the caddy I'd been carrying all over the house, I crossed into the kitchen and stood in front of the sink. Hot and cold compresses, those were what I needed to bring down the swelling on my eyes. I pulled out a clean dishrag and turned on the cold water faucet. I was still waiting for the water to get as cold as possible before I put the rag under the spray when I felt the regular brush of Princess on my bare ankles.

I glanced down at my little charge. "What's up with you, girl? You've already had breakfast and lunch."

She'd eaten really well both times, too. Just because I was too upset to eat didn't mean that I thought the poor kitty needed to go hungry.

Instead of sauntering away, Princess wound in and out of my legs in her trademark figure eights. I knew I was wasting water, but I let it run a little longer.

"You can't be hungry again. If you keep eating like this, you're going to lose your girlish figure."

To my comment, the cat answered a plaintive "meow."

"You can be as sweet as you want, but I'm not feeding you again until dinner." It struck me then that I wouldn't even be giving the cat her dinner. My aunt would be back to spoil her by then, probably feeding her albacore tuna off her own fork.

Again, the cat meowed, but finally she backed away from my legs. I expected her to disappear as she frequently did, leaving me alone with my thoughts and this squeaky-clean house. But anybody who understood cats knew that felines prefer to do as they please instead of what is expected.

In a single, effortless leap, Princess hopped on the counter. She barely hesitated before she leaned into the sink and started batting the stream of running water and then lapping at it with her tiny pink tongue.

For a few seconds, I could only stare at her. Had she really deigned to drink just for me?

"Well, it took you long enough." I eyed her suspiciously. "You know they're coming back today, don't you?"

Of course she didn't. Ruler of this roost or not, she

was just a cat, though I couldn't help but wonder if she'd seen me crying and just felt sorry for me.

Princess looked back at me before continuing to lap from her private water fountain. When she was done, she hopped down from the counter. At my feet, she stopped and rubbed against my ankles again.

I shut off the faucet, and then, on impulse, crouched down and scratched her tiny ears. Her fur was softer than I'd expected. Silken. Instead of skittering away or, worse yet, breaking into one of her hissing choruses, Princess tilted her head so I could scratch under her chin. And then she started purring.

"You were holding out on me, weren't you, Princess?" I said, scratching until she was ready to be finished and sauntered to her recliner for a nap.

I had this ridiculous urge to throw my hands in the air and shout "victory," but since I doubted that my new friend would appreciate the gesture, I contained myself. I couldn't help this tremor of accomplishment flowing through me, though.

Just as Luke had told me, I'd waited for her to come around, and she had. Sure, she'd waited until half past the eleventh hour, but she'd come. That I could win over a cat didn't automatically signal that the dreams I'd long since abandoned were within my reach. Still, it was something.

Trust and wait. My aunt's advice came to me once more, not so different from Luke's hints regarding the proper care of animals. Could I do those things now, letting go and letting God make sense of all my confusion?

"Okay, Lord, I'm trusting, and I'm waiting."

Turning the faucet back on, I wet the rag, squeezed it out and pressed it against my swollen lids. Next I switched the water to hot, dampened the rag again and repeated the process.

I glanced at Princess, finding her asleep now, dreaming the contented dreams of the seriously pampered. Her gesture today hadn't been a monumental statement. It was just the long-awaited acquiescence of a stubborn feline, but it was the best I had today.

"Cassie, I'm home."

I had been in the laundry room folding the last load of towels, but I hurried out at my aunt's call. Standing just inside the front door instead of the garage door where I would have expected her to enter, Aunt Eleanor looked utterly European, dressed all in black except for the multicolored scarf tied artfully at her neck. She had sunglasses propped on her head like a 1960s movie star.

"I'm so glad you're back." Rushing forward, I bent and wrapped her in my arms. When I could finally force myself to let her go, I stepped back and glanced around her.

"Where's Uncle Jack, and where's your luggage?"

"He'll be along shortly. He had an errand to run."

I realized that "errand" was code for him getting lost for a bit so that my aunt could have a few moments alone with me. Clearly, I didn't have any news to give to her; she already knew. The only way I could have beat this dissemination of information would have been to plan a press conference.

Because she'd never been one to mince words, she asked, "Do you want to talk about it?"

I shook my head at first and then changed my mind. "I guess this whole matchmaking scheme didn't turn out how you'd planned."

Eleanor led the way to the kitchen and poured both of us glasses of ice water from the dispenser in the refrigerator door. "I'm just sorry you got hurt by it."

"I'm not hurt," I began, but because she could see right through me, I didn't bother to say more. I accepted the glass from her and joined her as she headed out onto the deck.

Following her lead, I settled on one of the two chaises, holding my glass between my hands. "That had to be about the shortest engagement known to man, though I can name a celebrity or two with shorter marriages."

Instead of laughing as I hoped she would, my aunt turned serious. "You really love him, don't you?"

Aunt Eleanor was looking at the waves instead of me, but I still couldn't deny what she asked.

"I do. Too much for the short time we were together."

She laughed long and loud at that. "I fell in love with my Jack the day I met him. It just took a little longer to let him catch me."

"I heard that," my uncle called from inside the house.

"Then you quit eavesdropping and go bring in the bags."

"Yes, ma'am," he said, laughing with her, before he disappeared farther into the house.

After a long time, Aunt Eleanor spoke again. "I wouldn't give up just yet, sweetie."

For a few seconds, I traced my finger along the condensation on the glass, letting my thoughts travel a bit, as well, but then I stopped. "I have to."

"Why?"

I explained the discoveries I'd made about myself during my retreat at her home and my commitment never to sell out that way again.

"Luke will never figure out what's most important."

"Never is a long time, Cassie," Eleanor said with a smile. "And I've known Luke Sheridan since he was a boy. He's always been a smart one."

"He accused me of being judgmental and thinks I can't see any more in him than his late wife did."

"All right. There are a few subjects he's a little slow on—one being his own worth." Eleanor took a long drink and set her glass on the table before turning back to me. "But you should be able to relate to that."

"What are you talking about?" I asked with a frown.

"You've been trying to live up to your mother's and my brother's expectations ever since you were a girl. I know Melinda's goals for you sometimes became criticisms, but I don't think she intended to send you chasing for her approval."

I shook my head to deny what she was saying, but the truth of it was startlingly clear. No wonder I understood Luke's challenge when my own was so similar.

"Your mom and dad have been gone a long time now," my aunt continued. "Don't you think it's about time you just loved their memory and lived your own life?"

"I'm trying to do that. I spent a lot of time in prayer here, trying to get my priorities straight. And then everything happened so quickly with Luke. I finally realized the one thing I need from a relationship—time. It's the one thing he can't give me."

She smiled at me and pressed her glass against her cheek to cool herself. "Time. Isn't that the exact thing we often neglect to give to God?"

"Patience is definitely not my virtue."

"Remember Isaiah 40:31? 'But they who wait for the Lord shall renew their strength, they shall mount up with wings like eagles, they shall run and not be weary, they shall walk and not faint.'"

"Trust and wait, right?"

She grinned. "Trust and wait."

"I need to learn more Scriptures so I'll have one for every situation the way you do. I think I'll start by memorizing that one."

I would also follow my aunt's sound advice, even after I returned home. The situation felt hopeless, but it couldn't be if it was in God's hands. I would wait on Him this time. If it wasn't His will to heal my relationship with Luke, then I prayed He would heal my broken heart.

Chapter Fourteen

The four walls of my office at Blue Ribbon Elementary Academy felt even closer than normal as I sat at my kidney-shaped table surrounded by four second graders in the stifling post–Labor Day heat.

"It's too hot, Miss Blake," Lindsay whined, initiating a series of moans from Kayla, DiAndre and Michael.

I couldn't blame them. I wanted to whine, too, but I was the adult here, and I needed to distract them quickly. Indian Summer played havoc with education even in the best of circumstances, but it was a particular bane in schools like mine with no central air-conditioning.

"Just sit still and the breeze from the window will cool you off," I told her, hoping it was true. "Okay, we're going to work on our *r* sounds. Let's do our sound warm-up."

"Rrrr-rrrr-rrrr," I said to the group, all who were among my caseload of students with articulation disorders.

"Rrrr-rrrr-rrrr," the chorus of voices repeated.

"Now remember, I don't want to hear your old *r* sound. I want to hear your new *r* sound. Watch my mouth for clues."

"Row-rue-rie."

"Row-rue-rie," they repeated.

"Ar-ir-or-ur."

"Ar-ir-or-ur."

I went through the series of exercises, with each of the students repeating them together and individually. Later we would play the Concentration game together, using only *r* words.

"Ara-ari-aru."

"Ara-ari-aru."

"Who's that, Miss Blake?"

It had better not be another distraction was all I could think. I'd kept my office door open for the last few days in hopes of generating some sort of breeze out of this dead air, but I'd only invited more interruptions than any of my students could handle.

But the particular distraction who stood in the doorway wearing a sheepish grin was one I would have to allow. The children would let me make it up to them later.

I shook my head to stop my thoughts from spinning. Luke? Here in Toledo? I'd pictured him showing up here at school dozens of times since school started and at my apartment hundreds of times since I'd left Mantua two months ago. I'd imagined what he would do, what he would say and what I would say in return. Reality beat my fantasies hands down, and neither of us had spoken a word yet.

"Hi," he said finally.

"Hi." I doubted that our dialogue would win any best screenplay nominations, but my hands were still sweaty, and goose bumps scaled my arms.

"Sorry about the interruption at work."

"That's okay," I said automatically. Did he really think I'd mind?

"Is that your boyfriend, Miss Blake?" DiAndre asked, adding that second-grade distaste for the word *boyfriend*.

"Ooh," the other three chimed.

My face felt warm. Okay, none of the times I'd imagined this moment had I pictured an audience of seven-year-olds.

I turned back to the children. "Uh…well…no. I don't—"

But Luke cleared his throat to interrupt me. When I stopped, he lowered his gaze to my students. "We're good friends."

I studied him, waiting for him to say more.

He answered with a smile and a nod of certainty. "You and I need to talk."

I wanted to hear more, was desperate to feel that same assuredness that he had, but my answers would have to wait.

"These young ladies and gentleman and I have a date with the *r* sound right now. Any chance you'll be around in about forty minutes? I have a prep period and can meet you in the teachers' lounge."

"I came a long way to get here. I'll be waiting."

With that he turned and strode down the hall, his shoulders straight. Something had changed for Luke; I just knew it. I couldn't wait to learn what it was.

I reclaimed the children's attention and got back to work. All my nervous energy I channeled into today's lesson. First things first. The rest was, as it always had been whether I'd realized it or not, in God's hands.

Forty minutes and thirty seconds later I hurried into the teachers' lounge. One of my colleagues must have figured out what was happening and orchestrated the event because Luke was already situated at a table in the room, a soda next to him, but except for him, the usually busy lounge was deserted.

I sat across from him. "So you came."

"I came."

Louder than the words we spoke were the ones we didn't say. Luke had come *after me*, and I had hoped so much that he would.

"I'm sorry about the way we left things in Mantua," I began, but he shook his head to stop me.

"You were right."

"It wasn't about being right."

"No, it was about doing the right thing," he said, finishing for me.

I studied him for several seconds, but then I had to ask. "The right thing? I'm not sure I understand." Yes, choosing not to marry Luke then had been the right thing for me, but had it been right for him, too?

"Your rejection felt like a sledgehammer to my head."

I cleared my throat and straightened in my seat. "That was…graphic."

The sides of his mouth turned up. "It was also the wake-up call I needed."

"You mean about spending too much time away from your son?"

"Not exactly, but I don't expect you to understand because I never told you what was going on with Clyde."

Were we back to that? Had he driven across Michigan to tell me that he'd just been going through a rough patch at work and things would be just fine now?

He must have seen the doubt in my eyes because he chuckled. "No, we're not going there again. Here, let me explain. Clyde dropped a bomb on me. He told me with skyrocketing lumber and fuel prices, Heritage Hill Real Estate Development needed to do some belt-tightening on the new homes in the Wings Gate subdivision.

"For my boss, cost-cutting meant changing purchase orders and replacing higher-cost building materials that the home owners were paying for with cheaper ones. Mostly less visible things like the plumbing for the whirlpool tubs but others, too."

As he spoke, I couldn't help but stare at the table. How could I have been so insensitive? I hadn't listened when he'd told me the situation was bad at work.

"I'm so sorry," I said when he paused. "I had no idea."

"At first I had no idea what to do. My success in this business was so important to me. Too important. And then Clyde was demanding that I look the other way on business practices that went against my Christian values." He stopped and blew out an exasperated breath. "All that to keep a job that I'd just discovered I hated."

With that, all he'd needed was a judgmental girlfriend to nag him for spending too much time at the office. How fortunate for him, I'd stepped up for that task and performed it with flair. At the time, he'd said something about me on my high horse, but now I'd been bucked out of the saddle and the landing rightly smarted.

"Luke, why didn't you tell me? I might have been supportive and if not that at least a little less whiny."

"You did help me without knowing all the details—just by being you. Thank you."

I was laughing now. Here I was ready to give up helping people for their safety and well-being, and he was offering me an undeserved thanks.

"You mean my sledgehammer-to-the-head kind of help?"

He smiled, but he shook his head. "You showed me that it's possible to do God's will, even when it hurts."

At first I stared at him quizzically until realization dawned. He had understood that my decision to break our engagement had been about sacrifice rather than my heart.

"Right or wrong, I was trying to follow God's will." I had questioned and prayed about that decision ever since, wondering if I'd done the right thing.

"It was right," he said, answering the question for me. "It took me a while to understand a lot of things. Like why I believe that God could love me without my doing anything to deserve it and yet feel I had to work so hard to prove myself to the people I love."

People I love. My heart squeezed at his words. Did

he count me among those people even after our breakup? If he did, was there some way we could work all of this out so we could be together *and* do God's will?

"Do you have it all figured out then?" I asked him.

"At least part of it."

"Which part?" I held my breath, hoping for some elegant words that would be forever written in script in my wedding scrapbook.

He shrugged. "I quit my job. I want Sam to be proud of me for the man I am, not the money I make."

I nodded. Okay, it didn't have Elizabeth Barrett Browning's imagery, but it was poetic in its own way. At least for Luke and his son. Their lives would be better now. I was happy knowing that. It had to be enough.

"I also decided it wasn't enough just to walk away," he continued. "I told Clyde that I'd placed a few calls to an inspector friend of mine and a few of the new home owners, so he'll be under enough scrutiny that he'll have to toe the line from now on for his own good."

"That's great, Luke. I'm so happy to hear it."

This was what he'd come to tell me, I realized. He hadn't come after me to convince me to take him back. He only wanted to thank me as his friend for helping him to get his life straight. I should have been grateful. God had used me to help another person—what a privilege. But my heart ached. Sometimes doing the right thing wasn't enough. For the first time I understood that.

My eyes burned, and yet I wouldn't allow myself to

cry. God had a plan for me. Just because it wouldn't be with Luke didn't mean His plan wasn't perfect. Maybe if I repeated that to myself every day, the pain would lessen over time.

"I figured out something else."

I jerked my head up and found him watching me. How long he'd been studying me I didn't know. He was smiling as he reached for my hand.

"I decided I couldn't let go of the best thing that ever happened me. I finally found someone who really loves me, and I had to find a way to love myself and her the way we both deserve. With God's help, I can do that."

My heart was beating so loudly in my chest that he had to hear it. In fact, I was probably interrupting classes all through the building with this ridiculous pounding. "Her?"

"You." He grinned. "Were you thinking of someone else?"

Before I even realized what I was doing, I leaned across the table and kissed him right on the lips. He closed his arms around me, and I was home. I realized that from this moment on, home for me would always be wherever Luke Sheridan was.

The opening of the door and the chattering voices brought us apart with a jerk. Three of my colleagues who were coming in for their prep periods stood in the doorway, staring.

My cheeks burned as they hadn't since those sunny days at the cottage, but Luke just sat there grinning.

"Hi, guys," I said sheepishly. "This is my friend Luke Sheridan."

"Good friend," art teacher Stephen Oliver said. He

spoke for the group that included kindergarten teacher Tina Wyatt and third-grade teacher Brenda Lewis.

Luke stood and shook hands with Stephen and the two female teachers. "I'm just trying to convince my *friend* here to take me back."

"Looks like you're making a good case with her."

Stephen grinned at my frown. I could hear it now. They might as well announce this whole thing over the public address system because it would have reached every teacher in the building, plus the paraprofessionals and the other support staff by the time the final bell rang.

"She hasn't heard my whole pitch yet."

"Then by all means." Stephen ushered the other women out into the hall. He stuck his head back inside. "You have five minutes."

"I'll do my best," Luke assured him.

As soon as the door closed, he turned back to me.

"I've only got five minutes, so we need to make this fast."

"Is this like speed dating because I always thought it would be fun to meet twelve available men in sixty minutes?"

"Too late."

I'm sure I had some funny comeback on the tip of my tongue, but it fled the moment he reached into his pocket and withdrew the ring. No box. No decorator's icing. Just the ring that represented the promise I wanted more than anything to make.

"I love you, Cassie. I've probably always loved you, or at least the idea of you." He held his hands wide, the ring clasped in the left. "Well, here I am. I have nothing to offer you. I'm scarred and unemployed. But I'm hoping you'll take pity on me and become my wife."

At first, I couldn't answer but only stared at him, as tears streamed silently down my face.

Luke reached over and brushed the tears away with his thumb. "I guess I'm asking you to take me just as I am."

Suddenly, the tune of the traditional hymn, "Just As I Am," filtered through my thoughts. In the same way we had both come to God, as the imperfect people we were, Luke was offering himself to me. It felt like the most perfect gift.

"I wouldn't have it any other way." I smiled as the tears continued to fall.

For the second time this summer season, Luke kneeled in front of me and offered his ring.

"Cassie, will you marry me?"

"Yes." No misgivings this time, I felt at ease as he slipped the ring on my finger.

When the ring was in place, he stood and pulled me to him. I went willingly into his arms, lifting my face for his kiss. This was the man I'd dreamed about, I'd hoped and prayed for, and I'd known him all my life. I wanted nothing more than to spend the rest of it with him.

He kissed me again, a deep and passionate promise of the sweet intimacy ahead for us in our married life.

"Time's up," the art teacher called out.

Luke and I backed apart, but this time we were both grinning. I'd been caught sneaking kisses on the job for the second time in a quarter hour, but I didn't care.

"I take it she decided to give you another chance," Stephen said.

"Better than that," Luke told all of them. "She's taking the ultimate risk. She said yes."

I stared out the window at the dark lake, beating in barely controlled fury at the shoreline. One of the white folding chairs toppled, taking a perfectly good floral arrangement with it. The weather forecaster had said the storms wouldn't hit until dinnertime, and I prayed that just this once he was right.

Turning back from the window, I stared at someone in the mirror who didn't look like me. This woman was dressed in a prairie-style ivory gown with long sleeves and a high lace collar. She wore her hair in an elegant, upswept hairdo.

Because I hadn't heard her approach, it surprised me when Aunt Eleanor appeared behind me in the glass and squeezed my shoulders. "You make a beautiful bride, Cassandra Eleanor. But it's probably just the dress."

"I'm sure it is." I turned and hugged her. "Thanks for letting me wear it. I'm honored." It had taken some work, including lowering the hem a few inches, but we'd made the dress mine now.

Though she'd joked about it only a moment before, Eleanor's eyes flooded as she looked at me. "No, I'm honored that you asked. I wouldn't have been prouder if you were my own…."

My eyes burned then blurred. She didn't have to say *daughter* because I understood just how she felt. I loved her like a mother, as well, which I finally realized wasn't a betrayal to my own mother. God had given both women to me, and I could finally appreciate the gift in both of them.

I hugged her again before we both turned back to our images in the mirror and started repairing our makeup. Eleanor smoothed down her long lilac-colored gown. I had selected the long-sleeved sheaths for my aunt and Yvonne, my matchmakers turned bridesmaids, because I expected the wind to be chilly on the beach. Now I worried we should have chosen raincoats instead.

My aunt caught me watching the steel helmet of sky. "Don't worry, sweetie. The weather will hold out for your special day."

I shrugged. "I guess this was kind of a romantic notion to try a beach wedding in October."

"It's a romantic notion to have a wedding at all, isn't it?" She squeezed my shoulder. "Are you sad about leaving the school?"

I shrugged, uncertain, an ache filling my heart. I knew I had made the right choice, but that didn't make leaving any easier. "I hated having to say goodbye to my kids, but it was great that the school found another speech path to take over my caseload so soon."

"I'm sure you would have stayed until they found someone."

"I can always work with children in this area if I decide I miss it, but Luke I and will be busy enough just starting out."

"Hopefully, you'll get busy, making some new grandnieces and grandnephews for me, too."

I grinned at her because I hadn't even made it to the ceremony, and she was already clamoring for babies. My expression changed the moment I looked back out the window. Had the sky darkened again in the last ten minutes?

"Come on. Stop worrying," Eleanor said. "It's going to be beautiful." She glanced out at the same threatening sky I'd been observing. "As long as we do it soon."

Yvonne appeared at the slider then with a tux-clad Sam. "Are you ladies coming? You'd better hurry before this wedding becomes a washout."

"Yeah, Miss Cassie, it's going to rain," Sam announced, sounding excited about the prospect of seeing the whole wedding party drenched.

"Not on this wedding, it won't." I hurried outside, ruffling Sam's already messed-up hair as I went.

Down below, I could see Reverend Lewis, Luke, Marcus and Uncle Jack standing at the front, waiting for us. Those four plus most of our guests kept casting nervous glances at the sky. We descended the steps as gracefully as our gowns would allow. Because the sand was cold now, we all wore shoes today, but low, comfortable ones.

As soon as "The Wedding March" began, we hurried down the sandy aisle. I marched down the aisle unescorted this time, having chosen that for my second wedding I no longer needed anyone to give me away. Sam broke out in a run, and everyone laughed. When he reached the lectern area, Marcus pulled him next to him, resting a protective hand on his shoulder.

I smiled down at the sweet little boy, but then I looked up again, and Luke was smiling at me. My breath hitched. He stared at me as if I was the most beautiful woman he'd ever seen. In his dark tuxedo, he didn't look half-bad, either.

Would it still be like this for us twenty-five years from now? Would this amazing man still be able to take my breath away with just a secret smile or a loving look? Or would our love mellow into a warm comfort to span the years? I smiled back at him. I didn't care what the future held for us as long as I could share it with Luke.

When I reached him, Luke took my hand and leaned close to me. "Into every marriage, a little rain must fall."

Grinning at him, I whispered, "Are you kidding? There's only sunshine ahead for us."

The weather held out until just after the minister told Luke to kiss his bride. We didn't even wait for Reverend Lewis to introduce us as Luke and Cassie Sheridan but took off running hand in hand for the house. Our guests raced after us, with everyone looking spattered but not soaked.

Good thing we had chosen to have a small ceremony with only some friends from church and a few of my teacher friends from Ohio. A bigger crowd might not have even fit inside my aunt and uncle's huge house where we'd decided to have the reception. They would have been stuck out in the rain.

"Here's to the new Mr. and Mrs. Sheridan," Uncle Jack said, already at the punch bowl handing out cups of lime sherbet punch.

Outside the glass, lightning zigzagged over the water, and several seconds later thunder boomed.

Turning the job over to one of the other guests, Jack made his way over to Luke and me.

"Now you two sure know how to plan a party with fireworks," he said, his laughter filling the room.

Luke laughed with him. "My wife and I, we don't do anything halfway."

He wrapped his arm around my shoulders and pulled me close to him. *My wife and I.* I liked the sound of that.

Jack turned to my new husband. *Husband.* I liked the sound of that, too.

"So how are you getting along with our Cassie's dowry?"

"Uncle Jack, I wish you'd quit calling it that. It makes me sound like a head of cattle or something, available to the highest bidder."

"Sorry." Luke shook his head. "You're not available at all."

Aunt Eleanor joined the conversation then. "He's right, sweetie. You're downright off the auction block."

"Luke here was just telling me about the new project," Jack informed his wife.

Her eyebrow lifted. "Any new developments?"

I couldn't blame them for being interested. As soon as we'd called them to tell them that our engagement was back on, they'd told Luke about my "dowry," as they'd insisted on calling it. Since I was their sole heir anyway, they thought it would be fun to begin giving me my inheritance early by providing the funding for Luke and me to begin a small building company.

I smiled, remembering how Luke turned down the offer at first, worried that owning his own business would make him lose sight of family as his priority, but I'd convinced him we could work through the challenges of it, building the company together, slowly.

Now I could see the excitement in his eyes as he spoke of our plans to build a solid Christian business.

"It will be great for young families," he said. "Once we get the land, we'll build a community of quality, affordable homes where they can raise their families. We're going to build our own home right in the middle."

My uncle turned to me. "What about you, Cassie? Have you decided how involved you'll be in the company?"

"As involved as I can possibly be," I told him. "It's such a worthy venture. I can't help but want to be a part of it."

Our circle expanded as Marcus and Yvonne approached with Sam. Though we had yet to cut the round wedding cake, the boy already had frosting evidence on his mouth.

My new in-laws hugged and kissed the both of us before Yvonne moved on to Aunt Eleanor.

"Well, we did it, my friend," Yvonne said. "We've been friends for so many years, and now we're finally family."

Sam looked back and forth among all the adults. "Does this mean I have another grandma and grandpa, too?"

Luke reached down and squeezed his son's shoulder. "Don't mind him. He's just trying to get more Christmas presents."

My aunt only grinned. "Absolutely, sweetheart." She crouched down to his level. "So let Grandma Eleanor know what you just can't do without this Christmas."

We were all still laughing at that when Sam raised

his arms for me to pick him up. I lifted him, frosting face and all, up on my hip.

"And you'll always be my new mommy, right?"

My throat clogged, and I could see that all the other adults were as affected as I was. I needed to tell him that I wouldn't want to replace his mother, that she was the one who gave him life and who would always be a part of him, but he needed to be reassured now. I had a lot of time to help him to understand the rest.

I cleared my throat. "Yes, I'll always be your new mommy."

"Can I call you Mommy?"

"I'd like that."

While the rest of us misted up, Sam nodded, his questioned answered. He climbed down in search of more cake.

"Oh to see the world through the innocent eyes of a child," Aunt Eleanor said, and we all nodded our agreement.

After more well-wishing from friends, Luke finally drew me into the front hall for a moment alone. He didn't waste any time before pulling me into his arms and giving me the proper kiss that we'd missed by being chased in by the storm. Okay, it wasn't completely proper, but it was sweet and wonderful. As the kiss ended, he continued to hold me.

"I love you, Mrs. Sheridan," he breathed against my ear.

"That's a good thing, Mr. Sheridan, because I'm completely in love with you."

It was only right that this portion of our story would end where it began: with a wedding. I was humbled to have received this wonderful gift from God, our own happily ever after. The road we'd traveled had been a unique one. It had begun with a basket of flowers and a ring bearer's pillow, and it had taken many detours over the years; but the road and the God who directs all paths had finally led us here…to each other.

Sixty years and not counting.

Not counting at all.

Dear Reader,

As a reader and a writer, I have always had a love for fairy-tale endings. I want there to be an antidote for Romeo's poison that Juliet discovers just in time. I want Tristan to find a way to choose both love and honor instead of only honor, leaving Isolde alone. My story, *Flower Girl Bride,* is a reflection of my love for fairy tales, but in this story, as in our lives, reality invades on the path to happily ever after.

Would the journey to love be as sweet if we didn't face the trials handed to us by our past and our decisions? Does God allow us to undergo trials to teach us to savor those moments of pure joy? I believe He does, just as I believe that God has a plan for each of us and has a person He intends for us to discover along the way.

I love hearing from readers and may be contacted through my Web site at www.danacorbit.com or by regular mail at P.O. Box 2251, Farmington Hills, MI 48333-2251.

Dana Corbit

QUESTIONS FOR DISCUSSION

1. Like a lot of women, Cassie Blake is a huge fan of the old Hollywood version of romances. In what ways do movies depict honest elements of romance, and in what ways do movies incorporate fantasy? Give specific examples. What are some of the movies mentioned in *Flower Girl Bride?*
2. What is the irony in the fact that Cassie and Luke met in a happily-ever-after scene before they ever entered kindergarten?
3. Why do we as Christians easily accept that God could love us without our doing anything to deserve it and then struggle to prove ourselves worthy of love from the people in our lives?
4. Luke is convinced that his late wife thought of him as a failure. Why would that belief affect how he reacts to the discovery that his boss is participating in shady business practices? What is Luke's dilemma?
5. Sam plays a crucial role in bringing Cassie and Luke together, but Luke finds himself jealous of his son. Does Cassie give him reason to believe she's only seeing him to be close to his son? What is the attraction of a young widower? Is it a true pitfall for young widowers that they might date women who only want them for their children?

6. Princess is a major secondary character in the story. What are some of the duties Cassie is expected to complete for the cat while her aunt and uncle are in Paris?
7. How does the growing relationship between Cassie and the temperamental feline, Princess, reflect Cassie's character growth?
8. Cassie has an underlying love-hate relationship with her late mother. What are some specific ways that relationship is depicted in the story? How does that relationship affect the type of woman Cassie has become? How can she overcome the limitations placed on her by her past?
9. Cassie and Luke's romance is brought about by the matchmaking of Cassie's aunt Eleanor and Luke's mother, Yvonne. What are some of the setbacks the two of them face as they try to lead the two people they love to each other?
10. Many little girls include "playing bride" among their make-believe games, and by the time they reach adulthood, some women have specific ideas about the perfect gown, flowers or bridesmaid dresses they would like for their wedding day. What were your dreams about your wedding from your childhood? For those who are married, how did those dreams fit with the reality of your wedding day? For those still looking forward to that day, what details do you still hope to incorporate into your special day?